No Charge For Murder

A Frog Knot Mystery, Volume 1

Sloane McClain

Published by Sloane McClain, 2023.

.

Table of Contents

To my Fab Five - Nina, Pam, Brenda, Eunice, and Lisa. Thank you!

To my parents. I miss you and wish you could see this.

CHAPTER ONE

Periwinkle Manning hurried out of the hotel as quickly as possible without drawing undue attention. Unfortunately, she could do nothing about the trembling in her hands and legs. She stepped out into the humid night air of Georgetown, South Carolina. When the doorman asked if she wanted a taxi, Peri nodded. Almost immediately, a dark sedan pulled up to the curb. She didn't hesitate. Opening the back door, she climbed in.

The most handsome man Peri had ever laid eyes on turned in the driver's seat, his right hand resting on the top of the passenger seat. "Well, hello there."

"Hello. I need to go to Fishnets and Combat Boots. It's at Pawleys Island. Do you drive that far? Do you know where the nightclub is?"

His sparkling eyes widened. Then he grinned. "Yes, ma'am." Facing forward once more, he pulled into traffic a moment later. He seemed to fight laughter. She assumed it was over the club's name.

They had driven a few blocks when her driver observed, "You're shivering. Should I turn on the heat?"

Peri shook her head. "No, I'm fine." She couldn't very well explain that her trembling was from fear, not cold. Heat wouldn't help her. Peri feared nothing could—except perhaps a criminal defense attorney.

"A fan of female impersonators, are you?" he asked, following a few more seconds of driving.

Was she? Her head hurt badly, and she found it difficult to think. But she loved his baritone voice with its hint of Southern charm, even if it caused her stomach to flutter, which she didn't need. Nausea threatened. "No. I mean, yes. A... friend of mine is one of the headliners." Peri clamped her mouth shut before she said anything else. If she kept talking, he would soon know her life story.

And if the doorman remembered which cab she'd gotten into, he would pass on the information to the police. She didn't want anyone to be able to identify her.

Her driver was just too easy to talk to. It caused problems because Peri rarely had to guard her words. Before now, she'd never had a reason.

"You're an interesting lady."

Peri's blood froze in her veins. "What makes you say that? I'm dull. Boring, actually."

He laughed. Why did he have to have a wonderful laugh, too?

How Peri wished she could give him her number. It would be lovely to get to know him better. As usual, her timing was abysmal. In a week, she would probably be in prison.

Long before she was ready, the driver pulled up in front of the nightclub. Switching off the car, he got out and came around to open her door. Reaching in, he handed her out, steadying her when she wobbled.

"Are you sure you're all right?"

"Fine." After taking in his height, Peri yanked her focus back to what she needed to do. She opened her purse and searched for her wallet. "How much do I owe you?"

He smiled down at her. His deep blue eyes sparkled merrily in the bright lights. "No charge."

"There must be." Bending, Peri glanced into the front of the car, trying to see the meter or whatever it was they used to figure the mileage. She saw nothing but the dash. Quickly standing, she checked what she could see of the vehicle for a sticker with the symbol of one of the personal taxi services. Peri didn't see one of those either.

Horrified, Peri briefly closed her eyes before facing him. Her cheeks burned. "You're not a driver for hire, are you?"

"I am whatever you want me to be," he replied. Smiling, he pulled his billfold from the back pocket of his chinos. He retrieved a business card and held it out to her. "Feel free to call me anytime you need a ride."

Peri took the card and slipped it into her purse without looking at it. She didn't have time to figure out if he meant a double entendre in his last statement.

Something on her skirt captured his attention. She feared she knew what it was. Not for the first time, she wished she'd worn a dark-colored dress instead of the mint green one she had on. Following his gaze, Peri saw the smattering of brownish droplets that started a few inches below her waistband and continued almost to the hem in a diagonal.

He met her eyes, his narrowed. "Are you injured?"

Peri started to shake her head but stopped when the pain stabbed. "No, I'm just clumsy. I knocked over a plate of fries with ketchup." Time to make a hasty retreat. "Thanks so much for the ride. I really appreciate it. Gotta run."

Doing just that, Peri dodged clientele as she darted past the bouncer at the door and into the nightclub.

Theodore "Theo" Navarro took off after her. His moment of surprise cost him. When he reached the entrance, the bouncer stopped him.

"No breaking in line," the bouncer stated. She was four inches shorter than Theo's six-four, but she had about a hundred pounds on him.

"I'm following the lady in the green dress."

At the bouncer's ferocious frown, Theo realized how that had sounded.

"I meant, I'm with her," he tried a different tack.

Meaty arms crossed over an impressive bosom. "If the lady agreed, she would have waited for you—not run from you."

Theo groaned. So, the bouncer had seen that. He couldn't argue with her. He wouldn't get inside by being pushy, so he stepped out of the way of a couple waiting to enter. Reluctantly, he walked to the back of the line.

He could have gotten in his car and returned to the hotel to meet his friends, but his late-night passenger was an enigma. Theo wanted to get to know her better, and he also wanted to know what had happened to her. He didn't care what she said. That was blood on the skirt of her dress. He'd seen enough during his stint in the military to recognize it.

Something had frightened her and sent her running. If she needed help, Theo was ready, willing, and able.

If he could find her, that was.

Fishnets and Combat Boots was a popular nightclub. Theo stood in line for around eight minutes before he was again in front of the bouncer. The woman frowned at him but motioned for him to enter with a jerk of their head.

Theo didn't wait around. She might change her mind, and he couldn't have that. Theo hadn't even gotten his passenger's name. He doubted he'd be able to learn it tonight. As soon as he'd walked to the back of the line, the bouncer had called in a colleague and whispered in their ear.

His passenger said she was friends with one of the headliners. It meant not only was she probably a regular, but she was also probably well-known to the workers. Some of them seemed protective. The bouncer being a case in point. Theo didn't doubt they had warned his passenger of his continued presence. If she made a run for it out the back, he would lose her.

At least for tonight, but that wouldn't stop him. It would only slow him down.

The place was hopping. 'Aretha' was on stage in full command of most of the audience. Theo took several seconds to take in some of the show. It impressed him. The entertainer was good. Extremely good. They made him wish he could remain and watch the rest of the show, but he had a curvy brunette to locate.

Theo casually strolled around the perimeter of the large room. He didn't spot her in his first, second, or even third look around the place. There was no sign of his mystery woman. He would not find her this way. At this point, his best bet was to stake out the back entrance. In a perfect world, he'd find a spot where he could see both doors. Theo was lucky, but he doubted he was that lucky.

"**O**kay, babe, my last set is done. Let me change, and we can leave." Dean entered the dressing room in all his 'Dolly Parton' glory. He removed his wig, placing it on a model's head before walking behind a screen. Size fourteen stilettos flew over the top and bounced on the floor. A few seconds later, he tossed a white sequined gown over the screen to hang from its hanger. A six-foot-five man dressed in a Carolina blue t-shirt and cut-off jeans stepped barefoot from behind the screen. He folded his lean frame into a chair, opened a pack of wet cloths, and wiped the makeup from his face.

He caught a glimpse of her in the large mirror as he tossed the last cloth into the trash. Dean spun to face her. "What the hell happened to you? You're pale as white on rice."

Not ready to talk about it, not where one of the other performers could walk in at any time, she said, "I'll tell you when we get home. Are you ready?"

Slipping his bare feet into flip-flops, Dean picked up his billfold and slid it into his back pocket as he stood.

She was ready when he picked up his keys and held out his hand. She placed hers in his. It surprised her how desperately she needed to feel the touch of a friend.

Dean frowned down at her in concern. "I'm glad I'm driving. I wouldn't trust you behind the wheel. Did y'all drink too much?" Releasing her hand and wrapping his arm around her shoulders, he hugged her to his side as he walked them outside to his pickup.

Her head felt worse than a hangover, but she didn't say that. Peri relaxed slightly when he didn't press her on the drive home. Thankful to have a friend she could trust, she leaned back and tried not to start shaking again.

Though she hadn't noticed at the time, Dean must have broken some traffic laws. They got home much quicker than the twenty to twenty-five minutes it usually took.

He drove into the third bay of the garage, pushed the button to lower the door behind them, and turned off the truck. "Come on. Let's get you inside. I'd say get some alcohol inside you, but I think you've had enough already. I want you to tell me why you have blood spatter on your dress."

As she got out of the pickup, Peri looked at the brownish spots on her dress. "How can you tell?"

Dean canted his head to the side. "Army, remember? I know what dried blood looks like. It's not yours, so whose is it?"

"I don't know, but I'm pretty sure he's dead." Peri's shaking returned with a vengeance.

"Whoa. Back up. What do you mean you don't know who he is, but he's dead? How did a dead man's blood get on your dress?"

"I don't know."

"You told me you were meeting that old high school friend, Amy, tonight."

"I was supposed to, but the door was ajar when I got to her room. It didn't feel right. I knew better than to go in, but I thought Amy might have been hurt. I don't remember how far I got into the room before someone hit me from behind."

"Whoa! You didn't tell me they hurt you." Before she could respond, Dean moved behind her and searched through her thick hair.

"Ouch!" Peri yelped when he connected with the bump at the base of her skull.

"That's it, lady. We're going to the local urgent care and getting you checked out. If you get the all-clear, we're then going to the Sheriff's Department, and you're going to tell them everything." With his hand around her arm, Dean led her back to the passenger side and helped her in.

"Dean, they're going to think I killed that man." Peri knew he was correct, but her head felt like angry toddlers were jumping around on a trampoline inside. She understood she shouldn't have run. She also recognized that the head injury could be affecting her thinking processes.

"Newsflash, babe, if they've discovered the body, they'll have checked the hotel cameras and spotted you. Unless they have someone else on their CCTV footage, you're going to be suspect numero uno." He started the truck. As soon as the garage door opened, he backed out, swung the vehicle around, and headed for the twenty-four-hour urgent care in Georgetown.

Peri rode in silence. The more time passed, the more her head ached. To keep from thinking about trying to explain it to the police, she tried to remember every detail of her mystery driver.

Theo eased his sedan onto the road when the truck sped out of the driveway onto the highway. There was just enough light to allow him to see the shape of the two occupants. It was his former passenger and her nightclub friend.

Where the hell were they going? The guy broke a few traffic laws getting home, but he broke more heading back toward Georgetown. Theo's gut clenched when the truck whipped into the first twenty-four-hour urgent care they reached and rocked to a stop. Stopping on the road, Theo watched as her friend walked around to help her out and into the building.

Theo chastised himself for not making sure she wasn't injured. He knew it was blood on the skirt of her dress. Just because an injury hadn't been visible didn't mean she didn't have one.

The ringing of his cell jerked his attention back to his vehicle. "Yeah, Dalton, what is it?" He asked one of his two business partners, Dalton Blakeney.

"Where are you? I thought you were going to meet us for a beer. Jake and I just want to make sure you're all right."

"I'm fine. I'm sorry I didn't call to let you know. A pretty lady who mistook me for her Uber hijacked my car. She had me drop her off at Fishnets & Combat Boots."

"Are you serious?" His other partner, Jake, asked.

"Yes. If you're still in the bar, this doesn't need to be broadcast on speaker. Something is going on with this woman, and I need to know what it is. I don't even know her name. I followed her to her house, but there hasn't been a chance to look up the address on the county site. Can one of you do it for me?"

"Lay it on us. We're in my truck, so it's just the two of us," Dalton told him.

"It's a place called Frog Knot." Theo gave them the street address.

"Repeat that," Jake said.

Theo did.

"I don't need to look it up," Jake said. "I know whose address it is. Peri Manning lives there."

"You've got to be kidding me. Is Perry a female impersonator?" Dalton asked.

"No," Jake answered. "It's Peri with an i."

"Who's the impersonator, then?" Theo asked.

"That's her apartment tenant, Dean Robillard. Peri is short for Periwinkle," Jake continued.

"Are you joking around with us?" Theo had to have heard wrong.

"No. That's her name. Why do you think she goes by Peri? She owns the B&B at that address. It was and is her grandmother's home. When her grandfather, Guy Rutledge, died a couple of years ago, Hannah deeded it over to Peri, reserving a life estate. Anyway, Peri turned it into a B&B to afford the upkeep. I've hosted a couple of dinner parties there. I guess y'all don't remember. She's an old friend." Concern was evident in Jake's voice.

"I would have remembered her," Theo stated with certainty.

"Peri doesn't do the dinner parties. Her cousin and her cook handle those. What's going on?"

"That's just one thing I'm trying to discover. At the moment, her friend, Dean, has taken her to urgent care," Theo stated. "As soon as I learn something, I'll let you know."

"Do that. If something's going on with Peri, I want to know," Jake said. "I left my car at the office. Dalton's going to drop me there. I'll stay until I hear from you."

"Theo can call you just as easily if you're home. You might as well get some rest," Dalton said reasonably.

"He's right," Theo agreed. "If she does need help, you need to be rested."

"Fine. But call as soon as you know something. If I don't hear from you by morning, I'm going to call Dean."

"You didn't say you knew Dean, too. Text him and ask," Theo growled.

"I don't know him. Not really. Not enough to interrupt him at urgent care. I only got his number from Peri. The guy probably doesn't even remember I have it. Do you think he will answer and give a stranger Peri's condition?"

"I get it." Theo calmed. With his phone on speaker, he drove his car into the urgent care lot, parking next to a similar sedan. "Get some rest. I'll call if I learn anything." Theo ended the call.

He leaned back and watched the entrance. Most people would probably consider what he was doing nuts—if not stalking—but he'd never been able to resist a puzzle. Meeting three other guys in the Marines with the same drive was kismet. Once they were out, they'd started their detective and security agency. It was the perfect fit for the three of them that remained of their original foursome.

Sliding down in his seat, Theo tried to be as inconspicuous as possible. There weren't many vehicles in the lot, but the place was busy for the lateness of the hour. Seeing he wasn't the only person waiting in a car eased his mind.

Powering down both front windows, Theo turned the car engine off. Humid air wafted through. Sounds came through clearer. Traffic noises. The distant sound of music from somewhere off to the west. All the night sounds of a city enjoying its nightlife.

A compact car whipped into a parking slot. A couple of seconds later, a frazzled young woman got out. After plucking a crying toddler from the backseat, she rushed inside.

Nearly two hours passed before Peri and Dean—Theo was glad to have names—came out and got back in the truck. Theo waited until Dean backed out before starting his car. Because he thought he knew where they were headed, he nearly lost them. Instead of heading for Peri's house, Dean turned in the opposite direction.

Where the hell were they going now?

Theo eased onto the street. He kept a respectable distance behind them—all the way to the county sheriff's department.

What the hell was going on? First, the urgent care, and now the police.

Instead of getting answers, all Theo had was more questions. Jake might be able to wrangle some in the morning. Having an uncle who was the local sheriff could be handy.

The long day was catching up with Theo. Since he couldn't very well walk in and ask to be part of the discussion, there was no reason to stay. He needed sleep. He'd go home, text Jake, and get some rest.

While Peri was being checked out at the clinic, Dean called the sheriff's department to inform them they were coming in. It didn't surprise her when a deputy showed them into Sheriff Alton Calhoun's office, even at the ungodly hour of the morning.

He came around his desk to greet them. "Peri, how are you feeling?

"My head hurts. I feel like an idiot for leaving the crime scene. I should have stayed and called the police."

"Have a seat. If you feel up to it, can you tell me everything from your arrival at the hotel?" Alton urged her into a comfortable chair in front of his desk. He returned to his seat as Dean folded his frame into the chair beside hers.

"I was supposed to meet a friend from high school in her room at the hotel. As soon as I stepped inside, I was struck from behind. When I came to, there was a... man lying on the floor."

"Back up a minute, Peri. Did your friend let you in?" the sheriff asked.

Peri's brows wrinkled as her eyes narrowed. "No, I don't... No, the door was open a crack."

"Did you see your friend?" he asked next.

She had to concentrate to remember. That worried her as her memory was usually good, but finally, the memory surfaced. "No. Amy wasn't there."

"Is she okay?" The sheriff directed his question to Dean.

"No. The doc said she has a mild TBI. She's supposed to be resting and quiet for at least forty-eight hours. I'd have taken her back home, but she needed to tell someone what happened."

Peri wished Dean had taken her home. Her head ached like a son of a gun, and the nausea medicine hadn't had time to take effect. The doctor's questions had given her an idea of the cognition problems she might experience, but the sheriff's questions brought it home.

"I'll try to make this brief. You believe the man was dead?"

Without thinking, Peri nodded. Pain shot through the back of her head. It didn't help, but she pressed her hand against her forehead. "Yes. He wasn't moving. I think I checked for a pulse." She thought she had, but honestly, she couldn't remember. "I had to wash the blood from my hands, so I must have touched him."

"Where did the blood come from? Was he stabbed, shot, or was it from a blow to the head?"

Peri did not know. She couldn't remember. If she even knew. She only remembered that she'd had blood on her hands. "I don't know."

"Okay, just a couple more questions. What was the room number?"

Peri told him. That, she could remember.

"Did you recognize the man?" the sheriff asked.

Peri closed her eyes, trying to bring up an image. She couldn't. She could remember a male body but no features. Not even hair color. Opening her eyes, she met the older man's. "If I did, I don't remember. But he was lying face-down. I didn't turn him over."

"Sheriff, I think we're going to have to pick this up tomorrow," Dean stated. "She's supposed to get at least two days of quiet and rest."

Alton Calhoun nodded. "Have you called Mrs. Hannah?"

"No," Peri said. She didn't want her grandmother to worry.

"Yes, I called her from the urgent care," Dean stated.

Peri frowned at him. "I asked you not to."

"Honey, you don't scare me. Your grandmother does. I don't want her to be angry with me. She said she'd wait until tomorrow to try to talk to you."

If Dean believed that, he didn't know Hannah as well as he thought.

Alton stood, signaling the end of their meeting. "Dean, take Peri home. I'll make some calls and see if I can find out what happened. I'll try to let her rest until lunchtime, but that may depend on the city police in charge of the investigation."

CHAPTER TWO

Theo fumbled for his cell. He checked the time before answering. Eight-forty-seven. "What?" he barked. He seldom woke in the best of moods. Theo needed caffeine to become suitable for human companionship.

"After receiving your text, I called Uncle Alton to ask about Peri." Though Jake's voice was irritating so early in the morning, the subject garnered Theo's full attention.

"Don't keep me hanging. What did you learn?" Throwing back the sheet, Theo swung his legs over the side of the bed.

"It's a mystery," Jake stated. "Dean took her to see Uncle Alton to report a murder."

"What?" Theo hadn't expected that.

"Shut up and let me tell you." Theo heard amusement and something he couldn't define in his friend's tone. "Peri was supposed to meet a friend at the hotel. She arrived at an open door. When she entered, they struck her from behind."

"Someone hit her?" That explained some things, like her unsteadiness.

Jake ignored his outburst. "When she regained consciousness, there was a man's dead body in the room. Supposedly, that's where the bloodstains on her dress originated."

"What do you mean 'supposedly?'"

"Uncle Alton called the local police and gave them the particulars. When they arrived at the room, it was clean as the proverbial whistle."

Theo needed coffee. Copious amounts. He had to be missing something because nothing he heard was computing. "There wasn't a body? What happened to it?"

"Exactly what Uncle Alton wants to know. He's going to talk to Peri this morning and pick up her dress for evidence. If the blood on it isn't hers, it's proof someone else was there. Someone else who was injured. We know for certain that Peri was struck. The doctor she saw last night diagnosed her with a medium traumatic brain injury."

"Peri isn't a liar." Theo surprised himself with the anger raging through him.

"Of course, she's not." Jake sounded affronted and confused. "Look, just get dressed. I'm on my way over."

"Where are we going?" Theo needed coffee. Soon.

"Uncle Alton requested I join him at Frog Knot. I'm inviting you along. If you want to join us, that is."

"Where'd they get the name for the place?"

"One of Peri's ancestors. It should be frog army or toad knot, but the lady liked frogs but not the army, so she named it Frog Knot. Now do you want to join me or not?"

"Just get over here. I'll be waiting."

"Drink a couple of large mugs of coffee. I'm not taking you to Peri's when you're behaving like a bear with a sore paw."

"Argh," Theo growled. He ended the call and headed for the shower.

He was on his second cup of coffee when Jake knocked on his apartment door.

"Are you human yet?" Jake asked once Theo let him in.

After downing the last of his coffee, Theo set the mug in the sink. "Let's go." He followed Jake to his pickup.

Peri knew her grandmother wouldn't wait to check on her. She was right. Hannah Rutledge and her canine companion, Jigger, were waiting when Dean pulled into the garage.

Dean tried to tell Hannah that he could take care of Peri, but her grandmother was having none of that. At least Dean got to rest. Peri, not so much. Her grandmother was old-school, so she woke Peri every hour to ensure she was okay. By daylight, Peri was so tired that the phone's ringing nearly didn't wake her. She heard Hannah answer. Listening to the one-sided conversation, she heard enough to know someone was coming over.

Peri looked at her clock. It was barely eight AM. She could think of only one reason for such an early call—the police had found something, and either needed to talk to her or arrest her.

After getting a shower and washing her hair, careful of the lump at the base of her skull, Peri dressed in an oversized t-shirt and jean culottes. Her head still ached, and she still had balance issues.

While she showered, Hannah had closed her bedroom door. When Peri walked into the kitchen, five men sat at the breakfast table with Hannah and Dean. Maralyn, the family cook for as long as Peri could remember, stood at the kitchen island, frowning at the strangers.

Peri recognized the back of the sheriff's head, as well as his nephew Jake's. The back of the third head looked familiar. Her mind had to be playing tricks on her. It couldn't be, but it resembled the loose curls of her mystery driver.

When everyone turned to face her, and she realized it was her driver, Peri didn't know what to think.

Dean, sitting on the side with two men she didn't know, got up when he saw her. "Have a seat." He pulled out a chair for her.

"I'll fix you some breakfast," Maralyn said.

Peri knew she couldn't eat in front of these people. Just the thought made her already queasy stomach roil. "Just buttered toast and coffee."

"No coffee. No caffeine for two weeks," Dean said. "Doctor's orders. Milk, green tea, or hot apple cider?"

"Milk," Peri replied. It was too hot for a heated beverage that wasn't coffee.

"I'll get it for you. Go ahead and have a seat." Maralyn turned to the refrigerator and took out the milk.

Peri didn't want to sit. At least not at the table with all these people. Her grandmother sat at one end of the long table. The sheriff and one of the strangers flanked her. That left Peri with the option of taking Dean's seat or the one at the end, with him on one side and her mystery driver on the other. Feeling he was preferable to the second stranger, she took the seat at the head of the table.

"How are you feeling this morning?" her mystery man murmured the question.

"I'm fine."

"She most assuredly is not fine." Her grandmother frowned down the length of the table. "She is suffering from a concussion. From her pallor, her head still aches. If you paid attention to her stride, you would have noticed her wobbliness."

Peri frowned. She thought she'd walked fine.

"'I'm fine' would be my granddaughter's stock reply if she was bleeding to death," Hannah continued.

"Peri," Jake spoke up. "I don't believe you've been formally introduced to my partner, Theodore Navarro. Theo, this is Peri Manning."

"It's a pleasure to know your name finally, Peri," Theo said.

It took Peri's brain several seconds to realize he'd spoken and to compute what he'd said. She'd been too busy relishing the fact that she now knew his name. "Um, yes. You, too."

"Peri, before we go any further, let me introduce detectives Moore and Cruz," Sheriff Calhoun said. He quickly finished the introductions. "Where is the dress you wore last night?"

"I'll be recording this conversation." Moore tapped the screen of his cell twice before placing it on the table.

It surprised Peri when Jake did the same.

"It's in the hamper in my bathroom," she told them, confused as to why he wanted to know.

"I'll get it," her grandmother offered.

"If you could just show Detective Cruz the hamper, he'll retrieve it and put it in an evidence bag," Alton said. The detective identified as Cruz stood when Peri's grandmother did.

Peri couldn't wait any longer. She needed to know. "Am I under arrest?"

All heads swiveled in the sheriff's direction.

"No, you're not," he responded quickly. "We do, however, need your dress to test the stains."

"You found the murderer?" That would ease Peri's mind.

"No," Alton said regretfully. "Let me explain why we're here. Then Detective Moore needs to ask you some questions. Okay?"

Somehow, that sounded more ominous. Peri nodded. It wasn't as if she had the option to say no.

"After you left, I called the Georgetown police. They sent officers to the hotel. The night manager let them in the room. This is where things take a strange turn."

Peri's heart began to race. Something was wrong—besides someone's murder.

"There was no body, Peri—no sign of a crime scene. No blood. That's why we need your dress. We want to test the stains to see if we can find ones that don't belong to you," Alton explained.

"I don't understand." Peri frowned. It made no sense. Someone had hit her. She'd seen and felt the body when she'd regained consciousness.

The dead man hadn't walked off on his own. How could someone have disposed of the body and cleaned the blood so quickly?

But had she seen blood? She couldn't remember. All she really remembered seeing was the body. She'd assumed there was blood because of the splatters on her dress.

"Neither do we, Miss Manning," Moore said. "You have a concussion. Are you sure you remember the room number correctly?"

"Yes. I was to meet an old acquaintance of mine there. She told me her room number over the phone."

"We called your friend. She claims she never made the call and has no idea what you're talking about." Moore's tone was calm, but there was a hint of distrust, if not outright accusation, in it.

"The number is on my cell. You can see for yourself." Peri rose too quickly. Between that and the effect of the concussion, she leaned to the right.

"Whoa. Easy there." Theo caught her left arm and stood quickly to keep her from falling over. "Sit down. I'm sure Dean can get your cell for you."

"Sure," Dean said as Maralyn brought her a glass of milk and a salad plate with two slices of buttered toast. As the cook set them on the table, Dean asked. "Is it on your nightstand?"

"Yes," Peri said, letting Theo ease her back into her chair.

"Did she ever text you, or was it all done by voice?" Alton asked.

"No, no texts. All voice. I hadn't heard from Amy since college. She moved away after she and Jason married. She said she just wanted to catch up. We were more acquaintances than friends, but I thought it impolite to turn her down." Peri couldn't make sense of what they were telling her.

"Mrs. Hughes did say that while she wasn't in town, her husband was. She also said that you and Jason Hughes were an item during high school," Moore said.

"Jason and I were never an item. We dated maybe four times in a six-month span during junior year. Then Amy began dating him. They became a couple and dated from then on until their marriage, after they both graduated college." Drums pounded in Peri's head.

"You didn't like that, did you?" Moore's tone was accusatory.

"Don't put words in her mouth or act as if you know what she felt," Theo warned.

Cruz and Hannah returned, Cruz carrying a plastic bag with her dress stuffed into it.

Right behind them walked Dean. He handed Peri's cell phone to Alton.

Moore shot Theo a glare before turning back to her. "Mrs. Hughes said she hadn't heard from her husband since around seven p.m. last night. Are you saying you didn't meet with Jason Hughes instead of his wife? That you didn't get into a quarrel and kill him?"

Peri had trouble following him. She hadn't laid eyes on Jason Hughes since high school graduation. It had only taken two dates for her to realize they didn't suit. The last two dates were because she couldn't figure out how to get out of them. Peri had been relieved when he'd turned his attention to Amy. Now, this detective was telling her Jason was supposedly in town, and he thought she killed him. How could she kill someone when there wasn't a body?

"That's exactly what I'm telling you. I haven't seen Jason in years."

"How about clarifying something?" Jake asked the detective. "You found no crime scene. No body. Yet you're trying to accuse my friend of... what exactly?"

"I'm not accusing anyone of anything," Moore claimed.

"The hell you're not. That's exactly what you just did." Theo glared at him.

"I am simply trying to discover what happened last night," Moore continued. "One woman claims her husband is missing. Another woman claims she saw a dead male body. It would be an enormous coincidence if they're not tied together, don't you think?"

"A body which you have not found, and currently don't even have evidence was there in the first place. Peri didn't identify the man. The body is missing. You don't know who the person was. You have a man purported to be missing, but it hasn't even been twenty-four hours since Hughes was last heard from. And finally, you're jumping to conclusions and making a lot of assumptions without facts to back them up. The way I see it, at the moment, there is only one crime victim here. That is Miss Manning," Theo stated. "We know for a fact someone struck her from behind hard enough to render her unconscious and leave her with a concussion. Are you suggesting she did that to herself?"

Moore ignored him. "Are you sure you named the correct hotel?"

"If she's not, I am. I picked her up right outside," Theo stated.

"I thought you just met." Moore's eyes narrowed on Theo.

"We were just formally introduced," Theo replied. "We met last night." He went on to explain the circumstances.

"You also have her on CCTV footage arriving and leaving the hotel she named," Alton reminded the detective. He held out the phone to him. "Here are two calls logged exactly when Peri said she got them."

Moore took the device and studied it. "I see two calls from the same number. However, this is neither Mrs. Hughes' cell number nor her landline."

"My granddaughter is not a liar, Mr. Moore," Hannah stated with all the hauteur of a former teacher. "If she says she spoke to Amy Hughes, she spoke to Amy Hughes."

"You have the dress," the sheriff stated. "Unless you have more questions for Miss Manning concerning the assault on her person, I believe you're done here."

Detective Moore stared at the sheriff for a moment before giving a curt nod. He stood and looked first at Peri's grandmother. "Mrs.

Rutledge." He then faced Peri. "If you remember anything else." Removing a business card from his pocket, he placed it on the table.

"I'll show you out," Dean told the detectives.

"Jackass," Peri thought she heard Theo mutter when the two officers followed Dean from the room.

"Alton, what is going on here?" Hannah asked the moment they heard the door to the porte- cochère close.

Dean shut it with a little more force than necessary. Peri didn't blame him.

The sheriff shook his head. "I don't know, but it doesn't sound good. I'd feel better if the body hadn't disappeared. We might have learned who attacked Peri. As it is, unless they can match the blood on her dress to someone, we've got nothing except a lot of questions."

"The hotel must know who booked the room," Jake said.

"They would. If someone had, but they have no record of a reservation for that room last night." Alton told them. Reaching across the table, he retrieved Peri's cell phone from where Detective Moore had left it. He tapped the screen and put the phone to his ear. A few seconds later, he laid the phone on the table. "Whoever called you from that number isn't answering. Honestly, I won't be surprised if Moore discovers the number belongs to a burner phone."

Peri was confused. "Why would Amy call me from a burner phone?"

"To set you up while leaving nothing tangible pointing back to her," Theo surmised.

Putting her left elbow on the table, Peri rested her cheek in her palm. She picked up a slice of buttered toast with her right hand. "Set me up for what? The body has disappeared. There doesn't even appear to have been a crime."

"That's the big question, isn't it?" Theo frowned at her phone as if he could will it to divulge the secret of the call that started everything.

Peri nibbled her toast. It had cooled, but it still tasted good with all the melted butter. More importantly, it gave her something to think about besides the insane turn her life had suddenly taken.

"What is the plan, Alton?" Hannah asked. "I believe in being proactive. I want to get ahead of this."

Peri agreed with that. There was one problem that stood out. "But, Grannah, we don't even know what *this* is."

Her grandmother looked at her before smiling at Alton. "Alton will figure it out. He was one of my brightest students."

Peri took a bite of toast to hide her smile at seeing the tough, burly sheriff blush.

"If I'm going to live up to that glowing endorsement, I need to get to work." Alton picked up the business card Moore had left on the table and stood. "Mrs. Hannah, it's always a pleasure to see you."

"And you. Thought I would wish for different circumstances," Hannah responded.

"Amen to that." Pausing by her chair, Alton put the card on the table in front of Peri. "If you think of something, or remember something, give him a call. Just call me first, okay?"

"I will." Peri would be happy if she never spoke to Detective Moore again.

"Boys," Alton spoke to Theo and Jake.

They both stood.

"If Peri needs anything, call me," Jake told Dean. "Rest, Peri." He dropped a kiss on the top of her head as he passed.

Theo was the last to stand. He put a business card on top of the detective's. "If you need a taxi, give me a call. I'll be happy to drive you wherever you want to go." He followed Jake from the house.

At least he hadn't offered her a ride again. Peri thought her head might have exploded if he had. She wasn't used to come-on lines, so she still wasn't sure if that's what the comment from the previous night was. Now, he'd left her a second business card and offered to be her driver.

Peri didn't know what to make of it. The fact that her head hurt as if it was a bell someone was furiously clanging didn't help.

After refilling Hannah's mug with coffee, Dean sat between them. He grinned at Peri. "Girl, that Theo has the hots for you. When he wasn't looking at you like he wanted to protect you, he looked like he wanted to devour you."

Maralyn joined them with her own mug of coffee. She nodded her agreement.

When Peri realized her grandmother seemed to agree with Dean's assessment, her cheeks heated.

"I'll just put his number in your phone for you." Before she could stop him, Dean picked up the business card and added Theo's number to her contacts list. Then he pulled out his own phone and added it to his. When Hannah handed over her phone, Dean put it in hers. Not to be excluded, Maralyn also gave him hers. Putting Theo's card back on the table, he took a long sip of his coffee.

Peri made a face at him. Dean got coffee. Maralyn got coffee. Her grandmother got coffee. And she got milk. Well aware life wasn't fair; this seemed like piling on.

"Aren't you going to add Detective Moore's?" she asked.

Dean snorted. "Who wants to talk to him? I don't."

"Me either. I've already heard quite enough from that man," Hannah stated.

"I wouldn't have minded puttin' somethin' in his coffee to give him diarrhea," Maralyn added.

Peri agreed. For some reason, Moore seemed ready to pin something on her, dead body or not. It left her unsure whether to be glad the body had disappeared or worried it had. The detective certainly showed no concern about finding the person who assaulted her.

Even if she hadn't suffered some cognitive issues from the blow, Peri couldn't make sense of it. Either Amy called her from a burner phone and lied about it, or someone impersonating her called. The only reason for either call was to lure Peri to the hotel. If it was so someone would discover her with the body, then why move the body and clean the scene?

But Peri hadn't recognized the body. For murder, there should be some connection, or else what would her motive be? Thinking back, she hadn't seen the face. He'd been on his stomach.

After finishing her toast and milk, and at the urging of both her grandmother and Dean, Peri went back to bed. Hopping up with her and curling behind her knees, Jigger appointed herself Peri's guardian.

CHAPTER THREE

"Detective Moore is a bastard," Theo stated as he got into the passenger seat of his friend's truck.

"He seemed to take an instant dislike to her, didn't he?" Jake backed up and turned to drive out of the parking area of Frog Knot Plantation. "None of this is making sense."

Theo agreed. "I don't think this is over. That's what worries me."

"Oh damn, are you having one of your feelings?"

Theo inherited an ability to sense things from his mother's Celtic heritage. His friends learned of it during their many years in the service together. It even saved their lives a few times. Because of that, he couldn't very well deny he was having one now.

Jake glanced at him before turning onto the road. "Well, hell. I'll let Dalton know we're probably in for a bumpy ride."

Theo shot a glare at his friend. "I thought Peri was a friend of yours. Just how do you know her, anyway? Were you in school together?"

"I knew her through her brother, Merlin. He was my best friend all through school. Peri is three years younger."

"Merlin? Seriously? What is with her parents and these names?"

"I think they were going through some hippie phase when Lin and Peri were born."

"I've never heard you mention him."

"Because he's dead. The guy was brilliant. Full ride to MIT. Merlin and both of Peri's parents were killed during spring break his sophomore year. They were flying back with him to college. It was a small plane, and it crashed, instantly killing all twenty-three people on board. Peri was only seventeen. The only reason she wasn't with them was because her vacation was at a different time."

Theo couldn't imagine losing his entire family at one time. He didn't want to try. It wasn't any of his business, but if Jake were willing to share intel on Peri, Theo would learn what he could. "Her grandmother raised her after that?"

Jake nodded. "Her dad was a good bit older than her mom, so her paternal grandparents were already dead. None of his siblings were interested, as they were on the elderly side, too. Even if Mrs. Hannah would have allowed it—which she wouldn't. Her Aunt Gerry pitched in, but her career took her away most of the time. It still does."

"Gerry?"

"Yea, short for Geraldine. Gerry Rutledge. She's a talent agent. You may have heard of her."

"Yes, I've heard of her. Only I assumed, with the name and her handling mostly pro-football players and a few rock bands, that she was a he. I didn't realize how sexist that was till now."

"Her Aunt Gerry is definitely a force to be reckoned with."

From what Theo observed so far, every woman in Peri's family, Peri included, was a force to be reckoned with. What his dad affectionately called his "witchy" senses was warning him that Peri would need to be.

Peri reclined on the couch on the screened loggia that connected the back porch to the summer kitchen and garage. The two ceiling fans whirred overhead. Sitting nearby with her feet on the ottoman, her grandmother read the latest historical romance by her favorite author.

Jigger began barking several seconds before the front doorbell rang. Putting her book on the ottoman, Hannah followed her barking dog to the front door.

When her grandmother returned, Sheriff Alton was in tow. His expression told Peri he didn't have good news. At Hannah's urging, he sat on a chair near Peri.

Not wanting to feel at a disadvantage, Peri swung her feet to the floor and sat up. She waited impatiently.

"You look like you're sucking lemons, Alton. Just spit it out." Hannah resumed her seat.

"They got the analysis of the blood back. It's not human," he said.

"I don't understand." Peri didn't see how it could be anything else.

"The blood spatter on your dress is from a pig. It's not from a human. Certainly not from the body you saw," Alton said. "If not for the record of your concussion, Moore would believe you made up the entire incident."

"Why would Peri do that?" Hannah demanded.

"He believes for attention," Alton replied.

"The man is a fool," Hannah pronounced.

"I don't disagree," Alton said.

"I still don't understand." Peri frowned. "I didn't see a pig. I saw a man. How could the blood be porcine?"

Alton leaned forward, his forearms on his thighs. "Peri, do you have any enemies?"

Peri blinked. She glanced at her grandmother, who, after an arrested look, glared at the sheriff. "What are you implying, Alton?"

He sat up straight to meet her grandmother's stare. "This has all the earmarks of a set-up. An elaborate one. That usually means someone with a grudge."

"I'm sure I've angered people at some time or another, but not enough to do this." Peri knew it wasn't any of her friends. They got along fine, and she couldn't remember an argument about anything lately. She had tried to help one do some family research, but there wasn't anything surprising about what she'd found.

Alton had been observing her. He must have seen something in her expression. "What did you think of?"

"I helped a friend with a genealogy project. It's a hobby. But I found nothing shocking or salacious." Peri frowned. "At least, I don't think I did, but I just can't remember. I have records I can go through."

"Not for a few days. You're supposed to be resting," her grandmother reminded her.

Alton smiled. "I happen to know some people who can help. They're pretty good at research. The Marines trained one in computers."

Hannah smiled. "That sounds like a marvelous idea."

Peri wasn't following.

"I'll call Jake and see how soon he or one of the other two can get here."

Now she understood. "I don't need a detective agency to step in. I can go through my own records. Besides, even though we didn't find anything weird, I don't think my friend is going to want their name mixed up in this."

"Peri, you're not supposed to tax your brain. Or your eyes. Not for several days more. This can't wait." Her grandmother turned to the sheriff. "Call them, Alton."

"They'll keep everything confidential." Alton pulled his cell phone from his shirt pocket and dialed.

Peri gave up. For the moment, at least. One hardly ever won when Hannah set her mind on something. Deciding to pick her battles carefully. Peri swung her feet back up and stretched out on the couch once more.

Just because they were calling in Jake and his cronies didn't mean she had to share all of her information with them. There might be a bright side. She might get to gaze upon Theo's gorgeous self again. That might be worth all the aggravation.

Theo looked up from his laptop as Jake sauntered into his office. He eyed his friend expectantly.

"Uncle Alton just called. He's thrown a case our way. Pro Bono." Jake dropped into one of Theo's client chairs. "You're not going to believe this."

Dalton walked in, carrying three mugs of coffee. It was already hot outside, but their offices were air-conditioned. It meant coffee was always an option. Dalton set two mugs on the desk before taking the remaining seat.

Picking up his, Theo took a drink and leaned back, waiting.

"The blood on Peri's dress was pig," Jake informed them.

"What?" Theo and Dalton asked simultaneously.

"They didn't have to do a DNA test because the blood didn't belong to a human. Moore's fit to be tied. He thinks Peri set the entire thing up for attention. He threatened to bring her up on charges of filing a false police report," Jake continued.

"Idjit," Dalton muttered one of their favorite terms.

Theo agreed.

"Uncle Alton reminded him of her head injuries, and he backed off."

"What about the CCTV footage?" Theo asked.

Jake's eyes sharpened. "Interesting you bring that up. About twenty minutes before Peri arrived, the camera on that hall went down for about two minutes. Enough time to allow someone to sneak into the room and little enough time that the guard watching assumed it was a glitch. It shows Peri arriving in the hallway and entering the room. Several seconds later, it goes out for between two to three minutes. Around ten minutes later, Peri stumbled into the hallway and headed for the elevator. As soon as she entered the elevator, the cameras went down again. For about three minutes this time. Once they came back up, they never went down again."

"Someone had access to the CCTV feed to take it down the moment she entered the elevator. Inside job or hacked?" Theo looked at Dalton, their tech expert.

Dalton shrugged. "Inside job might be easiest, but I won't know without doing some digging."

Dalton's version of digging was to do his own hacking.

"How long will it take you to find out something?" Theo asked.

"Depends on the level of their security. Judging by what we've seen so far, I doubt it's high," Dalton replied, his brown eyes twinkling in anticipation.

"Someone or several someones are going to a helluva lot of trouble to catch Peri in something, but what's their end game?" It made no sense to Theo.

Jake shook his head. "Frighten her? Discredit her? If Moore arrested her for filing a false police report, her reputation would be shot even if the charges didn't stick. It could ruin her business. We all know how people love to believe the worst of someone."

"Why?" Theo asked.

"Uncle Alton believes it may have something to do with a recent friend that she helped with some genealogy or someone close to them."

"Maybe she dug up dirt someone wanted to remain buried," Dalton suggested.

Jake nodded. "Maybe they're trying to ruin her reputation so that if what she's found comes to light, no one will believe her."

Though he didn't like what he was thinking, Theo couldn't ignore it. "It would be a lot more effective just to kill her."

"True," Dalton agreed. "But that presents its own problems. Especially if they don't have the stomach for it. It could also cause a lot of questions they might prefer left unasked. I'd wager it's their Plan B, though." He looked from one to the other. "One of you better get out there and learn about this genealogy search. I'll get started on a review of the hotel's CCTV."

"Theo better go. Peri likes him," Jake teased.

"Oh, yeah. Do tell." Dalton eyed him with interest.

Ignoring them both, Theo stood. "I'll take it. You two get out of my office."

His buddies laughed. Taking their coffee with them, they preceded him into the hallway. As his friends headed for their respective offices, Theo headed out the back entrance.

If Jake hadn't offered him the job, Theo would have asked for it. He was attracted to Peri, and he had no trouble admitting it. He also felt the need to protect her. Added to that was the mystery of the whole thing. Someone was playing games with Peri—dangerous ones. Theo didn't like it. He was damned well going to figure it out.

Peri didn't bother to get up when the front doorbell rang. This was her grandmother's doing so her grandmother could answer it. It was either Jake or one of his two partners.

Peri still hadn't decided how to handle the situation. Private investigators had to be careful with their client's information. Peri felt she should get her friend's permission first, but the sheriff warned her that under no circumstances was she to let them know.

She had thought all morning about the genealogy projects she'd done over the last year, but her memory was still faulty. It played havoc with her concentration. If she hadn't seen signs of improvement, she would be terrified.

"Peri, one of Jake's partners is here to see you," Hannah announced cheerily as she came back onto the screened porch. The gorgeous Theo trailed behind her.

After all the weird stuff Fate had thrown at her lately, it seemed she was getting a reward. Theo Navarro had the most beautiful eyes

Peri had ever seen. Today, they were a Mediterranean blue instead of the deep midnight. The loose black curls just begged her fingers to sift through them. If she gave into temptation, would they believe her loss of control resulted from her concussion?

"I hope you're feeling better." Theo eyed her as if he knew exactly what had been running through her mind.

"I am. Thank you." No more nodding until Peri was sure it wouldn't start a new headache.

"I hope I can offer my services. The sheriff suggested we go over a recent research project of yours. Do you feel up to it?"

While Peri still wasn't sure about letting someone else look at her files, she had little choice. Besides, her research was innocuous enough. Though some people paid her, she did most for free just because it was a fun puzzle for her. Peri couldn't think of a thing that would have someone playing some elaborate prank.

And why and how was Amy involved? Peri was confident it was Amy who had called. She recognized her voice.

"Maybe you could just show me your files on it." Theo still stood.

Carefully, Peri swung her feet to the floor and stood. "I'll show you to my office."

"Since you seem in good company, Jigger and I have some errands to run. Theo, I trust you'll be here when we return." From her grandmother, it was a statement of expectation and not a question.

"Yes, ma'am. You may count on me," Theo responded.

Grabbing her purse and keys from the kitchen bar, Hannah headed out the front door. Jigger trotted along at her heels.

Peri tried to refrain from making a face at her grandmother's departing back. Errands, her foot. Hannah was playing matchmaker.

As she headed into the house, Theo stepped aside to allow her to precede him. Peri led him to the kitchen and then up the back stairway to her study at the front corner of the house.

Peri stepped aside and waved him toward her desk. "You might as well sit at my computer. I scan all my research notes into it to make them easier to access quickly. It'll be faster than going through the physical files."

Theo did as she suggested. He smiled up at her. "Smart to keep hard copies. You'd be surprised at how many people don't."

It took her a moment to get her mind in gear after that smile. "Uh, I worked as a legal secretary after college. One learns the importance of redundancy."

"Amen to that." He looked at the screen and then at her. "I doubt you trust me enough to give me your password. Yet, anyway. I'm going to need you to let me in."

Peri had forgotten about the password protection. A fact that annoyed her no end. Stepping around the desk, she bent over and rapidly typed in the short code. Using her mouse, she pulled up the main folder for the current year. Next, she opened the sub-folder for June. With one more click, she opened June, revealing two more sub-folders.

Peri straightened and stepped back. "There you go. These are the most recent. If you have any questions, I'll be in the family room."

She wasn't feeling up to sitting in the office with him. She'd be spending her time ogling him.

"I'll call if I need anything." He was already delving into her files.

Downstairs, Peri turned her favorite Pandora station on low. She stretched out on the long couch and closed her eyes. She was glad they didn't have any guests at the moment. Hopefully, the more rest she got, the quicker her brain would heal.

Theo wondered if Peri realized she had used her password in front of him. She looked better than she had on Saturday, but there were dark smudges under her eyes, and she was still pale. She was also still a little wobbly, as if her balance wasn't quite right.

He looked around the room. Behind him was a credenza he would bet doubled as a filing cabinet. At each end were two five-drawer filing cabinets in wood that blended with the rest of the furniture. In the front corner were bookcases on each wall. To his right was a window. In front of him was a door that opened onto the second-floor front porch. To his left, around an angle in the wall, was the interior door they'd entered through.

He forced his attention back to the screen. The month of June only had two files.

Two hours later, Theo had made it through both. He'd learned that Peri was very organized. She saved copies of every document, photograph, illustration, or any other item she perceived pertinent. She also typed up copious, yet concise, notes. Sorting through the files thoroughly took a lot of time because of the abundance of information they contained. So far, Theo hadn't run across anything that stood out.

If the answer wasn't in Peri's files, where was it? What could she have done to make someone angry enough to want to set her up for murder?

CHAPTER FOUR

When she'd first seen him, Peri couldn't envision a day when she'd tire of looking at Theo. She still couldn't envision that day. However, he was beginning to drive her insane. He'd become as bad a worrywart as her gran, Maralyn, and Dean. It had delighted her when her doctor pronounced her fit. She was still supposed to rest, but she was allowed to resume work.

Not that she had much. They had two couples staying with them and an elderly gentleman visiting his daughter and her family, but not wanting to stay at their house.

Peri copied her files from the rest of the year and sent them with Theo back to his own office to work. She needed her computer for her current project.

After supper, she grabbed her keys and wallet from the table and headed for her car. She needed some items from the office supply. Alston's Landing might be small, but it had just about everything anyone could want in the way of stores and restaurants.

While Peri was out, she had the crazy idea of preparing dinner for Theo herself as a way of thanking him for everything he had done for her. She shook her head as she put the grocery bags in her trunk. Peri had probably bought too many groceries, but Maralyn could always use what she didn't to prepare something for the guests.

She had the food. Now Peri just had to ask him.

By the time Peri returned home, it was late. Maralyn had left for the day; the guests had all gone to bed. Hannah had also gone to bed, and since Dean had the night off, he was probably up in his attic apartment.

Because she had several bags, Peri parked beneath the porte-cochère so she could carry them in through the entry room off the kitchen/breakfast area. Entering the kitchen, she sat the bags on the island and turned to go back for the rest.

That's when she saw the feet on the other side of the kitchen table. As she moved closer, she saw the leg, then the torso, and finally the head. Peri began to shake. It was Déjà vu to her incident at the hotel. This man, too, lay face down, with his head turned toward the family room. It took her a moment to recognize him. It was Jason Hughes. Amy's husband and the man the detective accused her of killing when there was no body.

Well, now there was a body, and it was in her kitchen.

Moving quickly, Peri grabbed the wall phone in record time. Because of her trembling, punching in the numbers took longer. Since her home was outside the city limits, she bypassed nine-one-one and dialed the sheriff's number directly.

Alton picked up on the second ring. "Peri, is everything okay?"

"No. No, it's not. I just came home from the store and found Jason Hughes' body on the kitchen floor." Peri's voice shook, but she delivered the information.

"Are you sure it's Jason Hughes?"

"He's older than the last time I saw him, but I recognize him."

"You're sure he's dead?" he asked. She could hear him moving.

If he meant had she checked for a pulse, no, she hadn't. She didn't want to, either. "Yes." It wasn't a lie. Not really. While she hadn't touched the body, his face was white, and she saw no signs of breathing.

"I've got people on the way. You should hear sirens in just a minute. I'm on my way, too, Peri. Stay on the phone with me and don't touch anything. Can you do that?"

"Yes." She could. Thankfully, she'd called him on the landline so she could use her cell to text Dean.

"Good. You don't have to talk unless you want to. I can tell you're there."

That sounded good to Peri, but she wasn't going to just stand there. Keeping one eye on the body, she emptied the bags containing the perishables and put them in the fridge and freezer. She doubted the killer would have touched the appliances, so it shouldn't count as messing up the crime scene.

Besides, if she could do normal things, maybe she could keep from freaking out over the dead body a couple of feet away.

"What the hell happened to me?" a male voice asked.

With a squeak, Peri spun toward the body, but it was exactly how she'd found it. Movement near the door she'd entered through caught her eye. Jason stood there wearing the same clothes as the body on the floor. There was one significant difference, however. The standing Jason was translucent.

She pointed to his body on the floor as Alton, having heard her sound of distress, demanded to know what was going on.

"I'm fine, Sheriff. A... a toad or something hit the screened door to the carport and startled me," Peri lied. "I'm sorry. I'm jumpy."

"Understandable. We'll be there in just a few," Alton promised.

Meanwhile, the apparition—that sounded less crazy than ghost, though not by much—followed the direction she pointed.

"What the...?" He looked at his corporeal body before looking down at his current form of being. *"Am I having an out-of-body experience? Cool. I always wanted to do that."*

Peri covered the speaker of the phone with her palm. "Yes, you are. The ultimate out-of-body experience. You're dead, Jason." Peri could have been kinder, she supposed, but darn it, she was having her own crisis. She was suddenly seeing spirits.

He looked at his prone form and then shook his head at her. *"No. I can't be. I'm only twenty-nine. I just got a humongous raise. My life is great! I can't drop dead now."*

Did he really not know what happened to him? "You didn't drop dead from natural causes. Someone murdered you."

He shook his head once more. *"Nope. That can't be right. Everyone loves me."*

Reaching for the nearest barstool, Peri pulled it out and quickly sat. As soon as she finished with the police, she was going back to her doctor. He'd released her too early. That had to be why she was seeing dead people. Not just bodies, but now spirits. She had to have gotten hit harder than any of them realized.

"Where am I?" Jason asked.

That was easier to answer than telling him that, obviously, everyone most definitely did not love him. "My grandmother's house."

"Why am I at her house?" He cautiously stepped around his body, coming closer to her.

"I have no idea. Don't you remember anything?"

Jason rubbed ghostly hands over his ethereal face. *"No."*

Peri perked up as she heard sirens.

Jason turned toward the sound. *"Who called the fuzz?"*

Was he serious? "I did. To remove the dead body from my home."

"Body? What body?" His head whipped around until he spotted his corpse. *"Oh, yeah."*

Jason had never been the sharpest knife in the drawer. He'd gotten by on his looks and athletic ability. But even for him, this was obtuse to a new level.

She was one to talk. She'd suffered memory loss from the time of her head wound, and now she was seeing ghosts. Peri needed to give him some slack.

She got up as the sirens screamed to a stop, but she heard the door to the porte-cochère being unlocked. It was confusing because Dean should have come from the family room door to the back porch. But maybe he'd gone out, too.

Only it wasn't Dean who rushed in the door. It was Theo. He left the door open, and several deputies followed him.

Peri stood and pointed at Theo's hand. "How did you get a key to my house?"

"Your grandmother," Theo replied, his eyes looking her over.

A couple of seconds later, one deputy walked toward her as two others went to the body. "Ms. Manning, can you tell me what happened? Did this man attack you?"

Peri's wide eyes turned to the deputy in front of her. "No, he didn't attack me. He's dead. I found him that way when I came back from grocery shopping."

"You can't possibly believe she killed him." Theo glared at the shorter man.

"There is a dead man on her floor and a missing knife from the block on the counter," the deputy responded.

Peri glanced at the knife block. One was missing. She hadn't turned Jason over to see how he'd been murdered. She'd only visually verified that he was dead. Stupidly, she'd assumed they had shot him.

"I don't think he's been dead that long. He's still warm," said a deputy who was checking the body.

Theo snatched her grocery receipt from the bar. He looked at it, took a quick picture with his phone, and then handed it to the nearest officer. "Time-stamped. You can check their cameras. You'll also have it on record when she called."

Maybe she would forgive her grandmother for giving Theo a key and him for using it.

Pulling an evidence bag from a pocket, the deputy held it up for Theo to drop the paper into. "We'll verify it all."

Peri wasn't sure why that sounded more like a threat.

Jason laughed. *"They can't seriously think you knifed me."*

Peri looked at the apparition before jerking her attention back to Theo and the plainclothes deputy. All she needed was for them to realize she was seeing spirits.

"You've got to help me, Peri. You're the only one who can see me," Jason said as he stood in front of the deputy and Theo, waving his arms and getting no reaction.

"What?" Realizing she had responded out loud, Peri clamped her lips together.

Theo tilted his head, his eyes narrowing as he watched her.

"I said that the sheriff and the coroner should arrive shortly." Thankfully, the officer had said something and assumed she hadn't heard him.

"You have to help me, Peri. For what we used to mean to each other."

It nearly took more willpower than she possessed not to give Jason the look of incredulity she felt.

"You don't want them to get away with it," Jason continued. *"They killed me in your house. If you don't help me, there'll always be the question of if you did it."*

"Do you know who it is?" the detective asked.

"Yes. His name is... was Jason Hughes."

Theo's head came up.

"The missing husband of the woman you claimed you were to meet last week?" Theo sounded suspicious now.

Peri nodded. She didn't want to say anymore. It was like they were handing her shovels, and she was using them to dig her hole deeper.

A woman wearing a vest with 'coroner' on the upper front left entered through the open door. After a swift glance, with which Peri felt the woman saw everything, she headed directly for the body.

As Jason walked over to observe the goings on around his corpse, Peri turned toward the door that led out to the porte-cochère. She didn't want to see any more of Jason—either his ghost or his mortal remains. She didn't want to look at Theo, either.

The sound of tires squealing could be heard over the muted sounds of the crime team. A moment later, Dean walked into the kitchen from the loggia.

The detective held his hand up, palm out. "Stop right there. This is an active crime scene."

"He's okay, Jackson. Dean lives in the apartment over the garage." No one had heard Sheriff Calhoun enter from the front. "Dean, go into the family room and have a seat. Theo, get over there, too. Keep your hands to your sides and don't touch anything. Not even the wall." Stepping to the end of the bar, he met Peri's gaze. "Run through everything you did when you got home."

"I brought in the first set of grocery bags and set them on the counter. When I turned to go back to get the rest, I saw the foot. I walked over to the table until I could see the body. I was sure he was dead. That's when I called you."

"Did you recognize him immediately?" Alton asked.

"No—"

"*Why not?*" Jason piped up, sounding insulted.

"—I hadn't seen him in years, and his face was partially turned away. But when I walked around, I got a better look," Peri ignored him. "I wasn't going to turn him over. I never expected him to be lying on my floor."

A rumbling, rattling noise announced the arrival of a gurney with a body bag folded on top. Standing, the coroner waved over the two people with it.

About that time, three of the five guests of the B&B came through the door to the hall and living room area.

"Sergeant, get those people out of here," Alton ordered.

A deputy immediately moved to intercept and move them out of the room. He closed the door behind him.

But not before Peri was sure they had seen the dead body. She couldn't wait to read the reviews of Frog Knot online. 'Come for the rest. Stay for the crime.' 'Free breakfast and a dead body.'

Alton walked a few steps toward the body. "What can you tell me, Sarah?"

Thankful for the distraction from her thoughts, Peri turned to the coroner and waited.

The middle-aged woman's brow furrowed. "I can tell you that he's deceased. That he's probably been dead no longer than three to four hours. He was stabbed in the chest. Whether that is the cause of death remains to be determined. As soon as I finish, you'll have my report on your desk." She headed for the front door.

"There's a knife missing from Ms. Manning's block," Detective Jackson pointed out.

They all looked at her knife block with its accusatory empty slot. Peri included.

"Weapon of convenience," Peri said before she thought about how it would sound. She'd obviously watched too many mysteries and detective shows for her own good. Not to mention the books she'd read. She tried to look calm as several pairs of eyes focused on her.

Alton nodded as if she had said nothing untoward. "It seems likely. Do you know how Mr. Hughes got into your house?"

Peri blinked. She hadn't even thought about that. She shook her head. "This door locks automatically if the door shuts, but we leave the front door open until eleven PM if we have guests. And we do."

"The carport door was locked," Theo stated. "I used a key."

Alton lifted one white eyebrow as he looked at him. He turned to Jackson. "Check all the entrances."

Peri watched the three officers fan out over the first floor of her house.

I don't know how I got in here," Jason said. *"I don't even know where here is."*

"It's Frog Knot," Peri responded automatically. She'd already told him that. His memory was as bad as hers.

Since the coroner left with the body and the other three men were searching her house, only four pairs of eyes focused on her this time.

"We understand, Peri. But we have to know if it was a forced entry or not," Alton said.

Or if someone had let Jason in. Peri understood what he didn't say. She nodded. Afraid they would read something in her eyes, Peri looked at the countertop. She needed to keep her mouth shut and stop giving them more ammunition to use against her. Even though she desperately wanted to ask Jason why he hadn't left with his corpse.

"So, you told me earlier. But I mean, how did I end up in your home? I don't remember coming here," Jason continued, as if she could respond.

Detective Jackson already showed signs of believing she was the killer. If she kept talking to someone none of them could see, she'd end up in a mental ward somewhere. Though Jackson would no doubt assume she was faking it to lay the groundwork for an insanity defense.

"Peri, you have to help me. I don't even know who killed me. Or why?" Jason whined from near her left shoulder.

Peri closed her eyes, trying to ignore the ghost. Hearing a bag snap open, she opened her eyes as Jackson walked around her bar carrying a large paper bag. He'd put on gloves. A moment later, he picked up her knife block with all the remaining knives, put it in the bag, and sealed it.

Maralyn would not be happy. Peri would have to go to Georgetown or Pawleys Island and get the cook a new set.

"They murdered me in your house, Peri. That makes it your responsibility to find out who did it."

Peri couldn't help turning and glaring at the spook. Was he serious? There was no way he was guilt-tripping her into looking for his killer. What she was going to do was get someone to sage the house and bless it. One of those should get rid of her unwanted houseguest. If not, she'd try to get someone to do an exorcism.

She jerked as a warm hand covered her clenched ones. Her gaze connected with Theo's concerned blue one. She wasn't quite ready to forgive him for his moment, or several, of doubt in her innocence, however.

"Do you need to lie down? How is your head feeling?" Theo asked.

It wasn't easy to concentrate on his questions while he was touching her. Her heart raced, and her stomach had happy little butterflies fluttering. "Lying down won't help with this problem," Peri managed. As for her head, she had no headache, but what would he say if she told him she seemed to be channeling Haley Joel Osment and seeing dead people?

"I and my partners will assist you any way we can," Theo promised. He gently squeezed her hands. Theo suddenly raised his head.

Turning in that direction, Peri watched the deputies return from the various areas they'd searched. She knew before they shook their heads that they hadn't found a specific point of ingress.

"All the doors are locked except the front one. No visible signs that anyone tried to break in anywhere else," Deputy Jackson stated. "It looks like a lover's quarrel gone wrong."

"Jason Hughes and I are not, nor were we ever, lovers. We dated briefly during high school. Until I discovered his body on my floor, I hadn't seen him since high school graduation." Peri faced the detective. "I don't know how he and whoever murdered him got into my house. Like most people do, I guess. Perhaps they did just walk through the front door."

"What is going on here?" Hannah demanded, coming down the kitchen stairs. Since her bedroom was the old billiard room, Peri had no doubt she'd gone up the front stairs and come down the back ones to bypass the deputy guarding the family room door.

"That would be convenient," Jackson said snarkily.

"That's enough, detective." No one could miss the warning in Alton's voice.

"But Sheriff, we should be arresting her on suspicion of murder. At least taking her in for questioning," Jackson argued.

"Murder? Who's been murdered?" Hannah asked, aghast.

Peri thought Jackson's suggestion was an excellent idea. She grabbed her purse. "Let's go. Let's get the questions and answers on record."

Jackson's eyes widened. He looked from her to his boss.

Alton nodded. "Questioning only. At least for the moment."

"I'm going with her," Theo stated, giving Peri a warm, fuzzy feeling.

"Me, too," Dean said in solidarity.

"Alton, what is going on here?" Hannah repeated her question.

"Fine. But neither of you may be in the room during the questioning," Alton said. He quickly turned to explain to her grandmother what had happened.

"Grannah, it's fine. I'll go answer questions, and then I'll be back. You're going to have to handle the guests. Okay?"

Looking dazed, her grandmother nodded.

Peri was glad of the support from Theo and Dean, but they were slowing things down. She looked at Deputy Jackson. "Can we just get this over with?"

CHAPTER FIVE

Two and a half hours later, all the questions they could think of had been asked, rephrased, and asked again. At that point, they had released Peri on her own recognizance—even though she hadn't officially been charged with anything.

Dean and Theo waited in a small area at the end of the hall. Both stood as she approached.

"You look like crap," Dean observed.

"Are you all right?" Theo asked.

"I just want to go home," Peri told them.

"Ah, about that," Dean began, then stopped. Whatever he wasn't saying, she would not like.

"Your kitchen is going to be off-limits until the techs finish," Alton spoke up from behind her. "They're still processing the crime scene, but they should be done by morning."

For the first time, the term 'crime scene' hit her. Someone had murdered Jason in her house. Her home's sanctity had been violated.

"Peri?" The sheriff called her name.

She looked at him and nodded. "How are we going to provide breakfast to our guests?"

"Maralyn can prepare it in the summer kitchen. They eat in the dining room, anyway. She can bring it in through the living room," Dean said. "Don't worry. It'll be fine."

"Come on, I'll drive you and Dean home," Theo said.

Alton clapped Theo on the shoulder. "Good man. I'll be in touch."

Not only was Peri exhausted, but she was also starting to feel shell-shocked. It didn't help that Jason's specter trailed her like a lost puppy.

Putting his arm around her back, Theo steered her out of the building. "Come on. Let's go see Ms. Hannah."

"I love Ms. Hannah," Jason said. *"She's a neat old lady."*

Peri gritted her teeth. She wanted to dare him to call her grandmother that to her face. Even though she knew he couldn't.

"Can we hurry, if you don't mind," Dean said. "If I'd known their interrogations would take so long, I'd have driven my truck. As it is, I may be late for work. I have to fill in for a friend who has to leave early."

"No problem." Theo led them to his sedan.

When they reached Frog Knot, three Sheriff's Department cruisers and a panel van labeled as the county's CSI were parked in the side driveway. As if she needed one, they were a visible reminder of the upheaval in her life.

Theo drove past them and parked behind the first bay door of the garage.

"Thanks, man." Dean gently squeezed Peri's shoulder before exiting the car and heading for the four-stall garage and his truck.

Theo followed Peri's frozen gaze to the vehicles in her drive. He wished he could throw his car in reverse and leave. Peri had been hit with a lot of weird crap over the past week. The lengthy interrogation hadn't helped. She looked exhausted.

"We'll figure this out, Peri. I promise."

Her lips barely twitched in a poor semblance of a smile.

Theo didn't know how she would react, but he reached out and gently closed his right hand over her nearest one. Because of the July heat, he had the car's air-conditioning on, but the chill he felt from her hand was an inner one. He rubbed his thumb back and forth across her knuckles.

"You're not alone in this, Peri. The guys and I have your back."

She faced him. Theo wished he could stare into her eyes, but one deputy leaving the house drew his gaze.

"But what is *this*, Theo? Why lure me to a hotel only to hit me over the head and fake a murder? Then wait a week and kill an old classmate in my home?"

Her use of the word 'lure' felt like a drop of ice water sliding down his spine.

Peri turned slightly to glare into the backseat.

Theo checked the rearview mirror. He didn't see anything, but he'd bet his last dollar that Peri did.

During the entire week he'd been at her house going through her files, she'd shown no signs of being anything but normal. The moment he'd let himself into her home earlier, he'd gotten the impression that Peri was seeing and hearing something the rest of them weren't privy to. Something had happened. And the only change was finding Jason Hughes's dead body. Theo's problem was convincing Peri she could trust him enough to tell him about it.

Theo opened his senses as his mother had taught him. He couldn't hear anything. Theo checked the rearview mirror again. He had the vague sense that he and Peri weren't alone in the vehicle. But for him, that's all it was: a feeling.

Now wasn't the time to ask Peri about it. Already on edge, he knew she would clam up if he suggested anything paranormal. Especially if it was new to her—which Theo felt it was. Before he pushed her, he wanted to confer with his mother.

Brenda Bridget Carrick Navarro was in full and glorious contact with her Celtic roots. Even though she was his mother, there were times she freaked him out. Theo didn't doubt she was already anticipating his call. He was surprised she hadn't preemptively called him.

After several minutes and a few more glares into his empty backseat by his passenger, Peri reached for the door handle. When Hannah rose from a comfortable chair on the loggia, he silently questioned the older woman's own clairvoyant abilities.

Hannah waited at the top of the shallow steps, her arms wide, and her black and white dog, Jigger, at her side. "My darling girl," Hannah said as Peri bounded up the steps into her grandmother's embrace.

Theo turned off his car and followed.

Hannah looked around Peri's shoulder and motioned for him to come up. "Come have a seat. I put the kettle on in the summer kitchen. We'll have some hot cocoa and relax until Peri feels like she can sleep."

As Peri dropped into a chair, Theo took a seat near her. Hannah went behind the bar at the end of the loggia beside the garage. They watched her prepare three mugs of cocoa. She returned several seconds later with a tray of steaming mugs. Theo wasn't sure about such a hot beverage on an already hot and muggy night, but if it would help Peri, he would not complain.

Peri did seem to relax as she drank the cocoa. When she finished, she got up and carried her mug to the sink in the bar of the summer kitchen. She looked exhausted as she returned.

"Darling, why don't you see if you can get some rest?" Hannah suggested.

"A murderer is running around. I'm not going to leave you alone to look after everything," Peri protested.

"She won't be alone. In fact, both of you go to bed. I'll camp out in your living room and monitor things," Theo said.

Peri shook her head. "I can't ask you to do that."

"You didn't. I offered." Standing, he took Hannah's empty mug and his own to the small sink in the summer kitchen. Returning, he extended his hand and helped Hannah to her feet. "Now, if you will show me to your rooms, I'll leave you to get some sleep."

Wrapping her arm around his left forearm, Hannah patted it with her free hand. "You are a wonderful young man, Theo. When this is settled, I want you to invite your parents to dinner."

"Thank you. I'd love to." Theo walked them along the rear porch and in through the living room door.

One deputy remained on watch at the door between the living room hall and the door to the family room-kitchen.

Hannah ignored him, pointing to a square alcove opposite where the deputy stood. "My granddaughter has the main bedroom there." She pointed to the door on their left. "I didn't feel right there after my husband passed. We remodeled the former billiard room. I feel closer to Guy in there." She smiled.

Theo bent and kissed the older woman's cheek. "Pleasant dreams, Hannah."

She smiled up at him before releasing his arm. Hannah went into her bedroom and closed the door behind her.

Theo turned to Peri.

"You don't have to stay. I don't mind waiting up with the police."

"I know, but you don't have to. I'm staying, Peri. There's no need for you to stay up, too." Bending, Theo kissed her on the forehead. "Get some sleep. I'll see you later."

She looked up at him with sleepy brown eyes. "Okay. Thank you, Theo. You're sweet."

With that less-than-stellar review of his character, Peri entered her room, closing the door behind her.

Theo smiled. He could live with sweet. It was a decent base to build on.

With time on his hands, Theo called his parents. He wanted to bring them up to speed on what was going on in his life. And, perhaps, get some insights from his mother.

It turned out Brenda Navarro didn't have any yet, but she would keep her senses open.

The police wrapped up and left around five-thirty. Fifteen minutes before Maralyn arrived to begin her day. She looked around the kitchen in dismay. As she gathered what she needed to clean the room, Theo washed the coffeepot and put the coffee on to brew.

He tried to help her clean up, but the cook was having none of it. She had Theo sit on one of the bar stools and tell her what had happened while she cleaned. By the time she was done, Theo had brought her up to speed.

As her sous chef, he helped Maralyn prepare breakfast. Five guests were staying at Frog Knot. Theo had seen three of them the previous night. Maralyn told him the two couples were both expected to check out. An older man visiting his daughter and her family was due to remain for another five days. Maralyn shared her concerns that the body was going to harm Peri's business.

Theo couldn't say anything to ease her fears. It worried him, too.

The first couple came down around seven-forty-five. They ate hurriedly, settled their bill, and left.

The second couple arrived around eight-thirty, just after the first couple left. These two didn't seem to be in a hurry. They lingered over breakfast when the older man joined them in the dining room. He had been the third person awakened by the noise the previous night, but he appeared unconcerned by what he'd seen. That gave Theo and Maralyn hope that the bed-and-breakfast wouldn't suffer.

When the three guests finished, Maralyn checked the couple out as the older man left for his daughter's. Dean, who made an appearance a few minutes before, helped Theo clear the table.

Theo couldn't wait for Peri and Hannah to wake up. He had some things he needed to attend to, so he had to leave.

Theo wasn't able to return to Frog Knot until near suppertime. He just wanted to see how things were going.

Parking in the car park near the garage, he walked into the loggia. Jigger met him, barking until she recognized him. She danced around him happily, only stopping long enough to allow him a pat or two. Then she ran and jumped into Hannah's lap. She was sitting in a comfortable chair, her feet on an ottoman. Two large ceiling fans whirred overhead, stirring the air and keeping it from being unbearably hot. However, they did little to squelch the humidity.

"Theo, I'm glad to see you. I wanted to thank you for staying last night. I'm worried the stress is getting to be too much for Peri. She's run to the store for Maralyn. I'm just enjoying the evening, waiting for Maralyn to call me for supper. I'd offer you some Key lime pie to tide you over, but it's too near the meal, so we'll save it for dessert. Peri makes the best I've ever tasted. And I'm not saying that just because she's my granddaughter."

"Thank you, I'd be delighted." Theo was surprised, but pleased.

They heard a car drive up and pull into the garage.

"That will be Peri returning with the groceries," Hannah said.

"Let me see if she needs any help." Theo walked through the summer kitchen and through the door into the garage. Peri was pulling two bags from the trunk. "May I help?"

Peri's head jerked up, and she looked at him in surprise. "Ah, yes. Thank you. You'll save me a trip." Picking up two canvas bags, she stepped back.

Theo picked up the three remaining and closed the trunk. He followed her back to the loggia.

Hannah stood as they entered.

Peri suddenly spun around and shouted, "Will you please shut up!"

Hannah froze. "Periwinkle Shenandoah Manning, what on earth is the matter with you? Theo hasn't said a word."

"Don't worry, Ms. Hannah. Peri wasn't talking to me. Were you?"

Wide brown eyes focused on him. Fear, embarrassment, and dread swirled in their lovely depths.

Hannah looked up at her granddaughter. "The blow to the back of your head."

Peri looked devastated by the comment. "I don't think this is a hallucination from the concussion, Grannah."

"Oh, sweetheart, that's not what I meant." Hannah realized her granddaughter had misconstrued her words. "I meant that the blow to your head opened something inside you that's allowing you to see things most people can't. I guess we should have told you sooner to prepare you in case it ever happened. The same thing happened to my mother. After a head injury rendered her unconscious for a time, she was able to see and communicate with dead people."

Most people would listen to that and think the people were insane, but not only did Theo have family members who would be considered witches and druids, he and his partners had seen unexplainable things during their tour of duty.

Peri's strange behavior lately suddenly made sense.

"You can see Jason's ghost," Theo said.

Peri nodded, her lips down-turned.

"Why so sad? Can't he tell you who killed him? We can figure out a way to get the cops to believe it."

"He doesn't know," Peri related. "He doesn't remember how he got to Frog Knot and says he didn't even know I lived here now."

Theo offered up some curses in his head.

Peri looked at a spot on Theo's left. "And he will *not* shut up. He's constantly blathering on about something. A lot of which is irrelevant to solving his murder." She glared, and then suddenly, her expression softened. "I'm sorry. I didn't mean to hurt your feelings. You just need to stop talking so much. If they think I'm crazy, I can't help figure out who murdered you."

Theo looked from Peri to the seemingly empty space beside him and back. It was disconcerting that she could see a figure standing beside him, and yet he could see nothing there.

"I thought he'd have to stick with his body." Peri glared at the space once more. "Apparently, that's not the case."

Theo fought a grin at her disgruntlement.

"Let's go inside," Hannah urged. "I think we could all use a drink."

Peri turned to follow her grandmother. "No, Jason, you can't have any. How would you hold the glass?"

Good question, Theo thought as he brought up the rear. At least he thought he was the last in line. According to his mother's stories, there were spirits who could hold things and even move them. He wondered what caused the difference.

Theo followed the two women into the large family room. Maralyn was puttering around in the kitchen. He could only imagine what the woman would say if she knew there was a ghost in the house. The older woman was superstitious with a capital S. She always wore her cross, which many people he knew did. They were all living in the Bible Belt, after all. But Maralyn Campbell took it to the next level. She also carried a plastic bottle of holy water—actually labeled as such—in her pocket at all times.

As Hannah went to a tray Maralyn had placed on the end of a counter, Peri carried her grocery bags to the kitchen and put them on a bar stool. She pulled out two more for him to set his bags on.

Hannah got his attention when she waved them to their seats.

Not wanting Peri to feel as if he was crowding her, Theo started to sit in one of the chairs. Peri surprised him by grabbing his hand and pulling him down on the couch beside her. His ego took a boost until he realized she was using him as a ghost buffer.

"He honestly can't remember who murdered him?" Theo had a difficult time believing the ghost had amnesia.

"I'm not sure Jason and honesty are on speaking terms, but that's what he claims."

A second later, Peri glared at the empty chair to her right. "Don't give me that. How many girls did you sleep with while you were dating Amy? Do you think she was stupid enough to believe you were just helping them study? Scratch that question. She married you, which calls both her intelligence and her sanity into question."

Theo watched in fascination and waited.

A moment later, Peri continued. "I realize that nearly everyone in this county is related if we look closely at our genealogy. But, no, I don't believe some were cousins you were trying to help. You cheated your way through math and English by copying Margie Foreman's test papers. You cheated through social studies and biology because the teachers were also coaches, and you were the star linebacker on the football team and second baseman in baseball."

For Theo, it was a one-sided conversation, but informative nonetheless.

"I can't believe you don't know who murdered you. Not to speak ill of the dead, but everyone did not love you. What were you even doing in Georgetown? That's a long way from Austin. You don't have family here anymore. Can't you at least recall that much?"

Theo waited along with Peri for an answer only she would hear.

Peri shook her head. The movement of her thick, dark hair instantly distracted Theo.

"Great. You were meeting someone. Who? Or do you remember why? That might help." Turning, Peri looked into Theo's eyes. "If I thought a whack to the head would knock some sense into him, I'd try to figure out a way to do it. Or if another whack would take me back to before, I'd bang my own head against the wall. Jason thinks he was in town to meet someone, but he can't remember who or why."

"Maybe his wife will. I'll call the sheriff and see if he's spoken to her yet." Theo pulled his phone from his pocket.

"Don't bother. Jason said he never told Amy his business... What?... Oh, he said if he told anyone, it would have been his secretary... Bambi Booza. You have got to be kidding me!"

Theo fought laughter as he asked, "Can he remember how to contact her?" He couldn't resist. "Great name."

Peri rolled her eyes at him. "Frat boy." She looked back at the seemingly empty chair. A second later, she gave Theo a cell number and Jason's office number.

Hannah returned with a tray of iced tea and two plates of finger sandwiches, cucumber, and pimento.

Peri signaled her, so Hannah took a seat near Theo.

After firing off a quick text asking Bambi if she knew whom her boss was supposed to be meeting, he took a glass of tea and a pimento cheese sandwich.

Except for the occasional comments from Peri to their invisible companion, conversation by Hannah steered to Theo's living arrangements. Learning he lived in a one-bedroom apartment, she informed him that she had a two-bedroom apartment on her third floor that just happened to be empty. In case he wanted to move out of the city.

Theo wasn't married to his tiny apartment. Nor did he like the idea of Hannah and Peri living alone while running a bed-and-breakfast. Dean was close, but not in the house. Though he hadn't known her long, he already cared for the octogenarian. Putting him in closer proximity to Peri would be a bonus.

"Grannah, he might want to see it first. It might be too small," Peri said.

With a crafty look in her warm brown eyes, Hannah suggested, "Why don't you show it to him, Peri? Let Theo see what he thinks."

"Okay." Peri got to her feet and looked down at him, waiting.

Theo quickly stood. He followed Peri to the kitchen steps and up to where they split after a landing to continue to two parts of the second floor. Turning, they walked past the door to her office and up a third set of steps to the top floor and the attic apartment.

At the top of the stairs was a wall. To the right was a closed door. Peri told him it was to the living area. She turned to the left, down a short hallway, and through an open door. They walked into a large bedroom. Two dormer windows with window seats across from them faced the back of the house. Against the inner wall sat a king-sized bed bracketed by two nightstands. There was also a sitting area with a comfortable chair, a table, and a floor lamp to his left in front of the floor-to-ceiling bookcases.

At the far end of the room was a closed door and a partially open, sliding barn-type door. Peri waved a hand toward it, so Theo walked over. Opening the door, he found a generous closet. Looking through the open barn door, he found the bathroom. It was small, but not too small. Vanity and sink, commode, and a shower-tub combo. Perfect for him.

He walked back out to the bedroom.

Peri led him back through the hall to the other side of the house. There was a huge rectangular room with three dormers that faced the front of the house and at least one he could see at the far end. At this end, near the stairs, was a small kitchen with a microwave but no stove.

At each end, there was a door in the wall.

"It's a storage room at this end. A second bedroom and bath at the other," Peri said when he raised an eyebrow.

"Nice," he told Peri.

"Are you seriously considering this?" She asked him as she headed for the stairs.

"Of course I am. I grew up in the country. I don't like the noise of city apartment living." Theo liked the size of the living area. There was plenty of room for his furniture. Much more space than he had in his current place. "Even the tiny kitchen area."

Peri grinned. "Grannah would hope that you'd join us for meals. If you don't want to do that, she'd let you use her kitchen." Tilting her head, she eyed him. "Still think it's a good idea?"

Theo laughed. "Absolutely. It's perfect. I hate to cook. And my mother will love it. However, that may break the deal with Hannah, as I'll have to give Mom her phone number. And I'm sure she'll be calling to make sure I'm behaving and to check up on me."

Peri stared at him for a moment before laughing, too. "I hope you have a gym membership, then, because Grannah and Maralyn are superb cooks who will ensure you're well-fed." Her gaze traveled to his feet and back up. "I'd hate for you to lose that gorgeous phys..." Her eyes widened as she realized what she was saying.

Spinning on her heel, she started for the stairs. "Okay, then, let's go tell Grannah she has a new tenant."

He passed the stairs to point to a door they'd passed earlier. "Wait, what is this?" he asked as he walked over to investigate.

"Elevator."

"Really?" Theo opened the door to find that it was, indeed, an elevator. "Cool." He raised an eyebrow at her. "You weren't going to tell me about it?"

Peri grinned, heading down the stairs. "I wanted to see if you'd want the place without knowing it wouldn't be hard to get your stuff up here."

Chuckling, Theo followed her. When they reached the second floor, he asked, "Have you had many tenants for this apartment?"

"No. You're the first," Peri informed him.

"Did Jason follow us?" Theo was curious.

"Yes. I hope he hasn't somehow bonded to me. If this keeps up, I'm bound to slip, and then people are going to think I've lost my mind." She stopped to glare at a spot to her left. "No, I don't want you hanging around for old time's sake. Why don't you go haunt your wife?"

"What's his answer for that?" Theo wished he could at least hear the ghost.

Peri turned to him. "He says it's because he doesn't like her, and he was planning to divorce her." She rolled her eyes.

Theo jerked to attention. "Divorces are often motives for murder."

Peri's eyes widened as the truth of his statement settled in. She looked to where Theo assumed Jason's spirit stood before looking back at him. "He says Amy doesn't know yet, and besides, he doesn't believe she has the guts to murder him."

"She wouldn't need either, would she, if she hired someone?" he suggested.

Peri looked at him again. "You have a devious mind, Theo Navarro. I like that."

Theo smiled back. He liked that she liked it.

"How do we discover if she did?" Peri asked.

"Ah, to quote Shakespeare, 'there's the rub.' Third-party murders are harder to prove. And harder to discover in the first place. We'd need to find the killer and see if he or she will turn on the person who hired them."

"But can't Amy lead us to the killer instead of the other way round? If she is behind it."

"Perhaps. But she'd have to be stupid enough to have some direct contact with them through a medium the police can connect with her."

Peri gritted her teeth for a moment. "Jason says to check her cell phone."

"Whoever called you, called from a burner phone. Does Jason think Amy would be smart enough to buy and use one?" Theo tried not to laugh at Peri's aggrieved expression.

A moment later, she shook her head.

Interesting. Either Amy was a lot smarter than Jason gave her credit for, or someone was setting up both Peri and Amy. Why? Convenience? If so, Theo thought the killer must be an acquaintance of all of them. They'd gone through high school together, which made for quite a bit of suspects. Theo wanted to get his hands on the yearbooks for all their high school years. He couldn't count on the person having graduated with them.

Peri headed down the last flight of stairs. "If you need help to move, Dean has a pickup. We could help."

Theo's brows drew together as he twisted up one side of his mouth. Now, he questioned the type of relationship Peri and Dean had. "That would be great. Jake and Dalton have trucks, too. I don't have that much stuff. Only a little furniture, so with three trucks and my car, we could probably move everything in one trip."

Peri glanced over her shoulder at him. "But you have a TV sixty inches or larger, don't you?"

"Of course. Doesn't every red-blooded male?" Theo grinned at her. He followed her into the kitchen.

Hannah smiled at them. "What do you think?" She sat at the kitchen table.

Theo walked over and squatted in front of her. "I think you have a new tenant if you're sure you want me. I must warn you that my mother will call you to check up on me."

Hannah leaned forward, clasping the hand he held out between both of hers. "I am delighted. And I will be delighted to talk with your mother. My kitchen is your kitchen. I'll make sure Maralyn cleans you off a shelf in the fridge."

"Sounds great. The small upstairs fridge should be plenty for my needs. I can move in this weekend, if that's okay."

"It's wonderful. Begin moving your things in whenever you like."

CHAPTER SIX

By the time Peri could go to bed, she was exhausted. She barely had the energy to change into her jammies and crawl into bed. The familiarity of the room helped calm her.

It had taken the threat of exorcising him to make Jason swear to remain in the family room. Peri wouldn't have gotten any sleep knowing he was haunting the entire house. Who would have thought a ghost would be afraid to be left alone?

The moment her head hit the pillow, her mind went full throttle, trying to make sense of everything. Peri doubted she could. She didn't have enough pieces yet. The incident at the hotel was connected. It had to be, but how? Why pretend to kill someone and then later kill someone? And why drag her into it?

Amy claimed she hadn't called, but Peri recognized her voice. It didn't mean someone couldn't have imitated her, but again, why? And who?

Peri could understand someone trying to set up Amy. The spouse was nearly always the first suspect. There had to be a reason someone had murdered Jason so far from home. For Amy to be an accessory, the police would have to prove a connection. So far, they had found none. At least none they were sharing. That left Peri as the prime suspect since she knew him, and his body was discovered in her home with her kitchen knife still in him.

Except Peri didn't have a motive. She hadn't seen Jason in around eleven years. What would her reason be to kill him now?

Maybe she was coming at it wrong. Maybe Peri needed to begin with why anyone would want Jason dead. He could be a jerk a lot of the time, but he wasn't mean or cruel. Peri supposed he could have made enemies through his work. Peri didn't even know what he did for a living. She doubted Amy would tell her. She would ask Jason in the morning. Hopefully, his murder hadn't wiped all his memories. He remembered his wife and his past, as far as Peri knew. She hoped he could tell her about his work.

Peri closed her eyes and willed herself to sleep. Visions of a handsome face danced behind her closed eyelids. Theo had the most beautiful deep blue eyes.

It wasn't just his eyes—or even his gorgeous body. Theo was genuinely nice. Peri was used to people loving her grandmother. She'd met very few in her life who didn't. Theo, though, already treated Hannah as if she was a member of his family. Though she would never admit it to him, Peri felt better knowing that Theo would soon be living in the house. She knew her Aunt Gerry would, too.

It surprised her that she hadn't heard from her aunt. Gerry called Grannah every day. Hannah had undoubtedly told her daughter everything going on. It wouldn't surprise Peri if her aunt appeared before long.

Peri's Aunt Gerry was an agent and promoter for pro ball players, as well as a couple of rock bands. She was currently trying to help two of her football clients secure positions with teams before the pre-season began. That meant she was busy. However, that wouldn't stop her from flying in for a day or two.

Turning onto her side as she heard the air-conditioning whir to life, Peri plumped her pillow. This time, when she put her head back down, she succumbed to the exhaustion pulling at her.

Thursday, Peri and Hannah returned to Frog Knot after a morning of taking Hannah shopping. Peri froze while they were crossing the loggia.

"Are you okay, honey?" Grannah asked.

Peri smiled as she nodded. She didn't want her grandmother to realize that there were times when fear struck her when approaching the murder scene. Especially when the murderer hadn't been caught, and they didn't know who the heck the killer was. Still, it was home. Peri wouldn't allow something beyond her control to run her out. It wasn't as if there was blood everywhere.

Peri drew up short. Why wasn't there a pool of blood under Jason's body when she found him? She supposed it was possible it had soaked into his shirt. Or maybe the knife somehow blocked it? What she knew about knife wounds wouldn't even fill a thimble. Now she was eager to get inside and talk to Maralyn.

"Peri?"

"Sorry, Grannah. Just thinking. I'm fine.?"

"Well, if you're not, you will be after eating some lunch," Maralyn spoke up from the doorway. "Now get in here."

No matter how brave a face she put on for her grandmother, Peri was scared.

A pouting spirit silently following them around all morning hadn't helped at all. She wasn't sure what was wrong with him. Peri thought it might be because his short-term memory was holier than Swiss cheese. She knew Jason was angry because he couldn't remember his own murder. She would be, too, in his shoes.

While it annoyed her that he refused to speak, Peri admitted she was enjoying the silence.

As they entered the house, they found Dean and Theo already seated at the kitchen table.

"Still have your ghost shadow?" Theo asked once she closed the car door.

Peri looked across to where—for her at least—a diaphanous version of Jason stood beside the porch door, his gaze on the spot where his body had been found. "Yes, he's here."

"Whoa." Dean held up his hand. "Rewind. What are you talking about?"

Maralyn dropped the spoon she had been holding, and it bounced on the floor, splattering what looked like cake batter.

Peri had forgotten Dean and Maralyn didn't know. "Fun aftereffect of my concussion. I can now see dead people. Or rather, one dead person. Jason Hughes."

Peri hoped she didn't start seeing more. One was more than enough.

Dean looked at her for a moment and then laughed. "You're joking, right?" When she just looked at him, he turned to Theo. "Oh, come on, you're telling me that ghosts are real?"

Maralyn obviously believed it. She had her cross in one hand and the bottle of holy water she always carried clutched in her other.

"I can't say for more than Jason, but either he's real, or the concussion left me crazy. Believe me, I haven't ruled that out."

"You're not crazy," Theo stated.

Peri hugged his confidence to her heart.

"You ain't crazy. You're just like your great-grandma. That woman was a legend around these parts," Maralyn added.

"You don't seem too happy about it," Dean observed.

"I'm not. He doesn't remember who killed him. He doesn't remember coming here. As far as I can tell, there are no advantages to seeing him. Just aggravation," she tried to explain.

"Hey, I'm already dead. There's no need to be rude about it." Jason came out of his stupor to glare at her.

"You're right. I'm sorry," Peri told Jason.

"You're sorry for what?" Dean asked. Then his eyes widened. "OMG, you were talking to the ghost!"

Maralyn's eyes widened as she stared at what, for her, was an empty space.

Peri rolled her eyes at Jason's complaint, but she relayed it. "Jason wants us to use his name. He doesn't like being referred to as the ghost or the spirit."

"My bad. Sorry, dude," Dean apologized.

Peri stared at Maralyn and gave herself a mental shake. She couldn't delay forever. "Maralyn, I need to ask you something."

The older woman nodded, but watched her warily.

"Did you have to clean up much blood the morning after I found the body?"

Maralyn's eyes widened more. "I didn't see any blood." She thought for a moment and then added, "There was a brown spot near the table. About the size of a half-dollar. I just thought it was something the cops dropped."

"Where was the blood? If they murdered Jason here, shouldn't there be more blood?" She turned to Theo. "The police don't clean up, do they?" She pointed to the spot on the rug that stuck out around the table.

"It depends. Sometimes they do, but this hadn't been cleaned," Theo stated. "This isn't right." He squatted, first visually inspecting the hardwood floor and area rug and then touching the rug.

"Jason wants to know what it means," Peri relayed. "So do I."

"Me, too," Dean added.

Maralyn and Hannah both nodded.

Theo stood and looked down into her eyes. "My guess is that he was killed somewhere else, and then the body dumped here."

Peri looked at Jason.

He shrugged and shook his head. *"Sorry, I can't help you. If I could manipulate the physical plane, I wouldn't believe I was dead. I'm still not convinced I'm not caught in some nightmare."*

Peri wished she could tell him he was. "If it is, I wouldn't know, would I? Because I'd be caught up in it, too." It was the best she could do.

Jason smiled, so it must have been enough. *"You're right. You're just part of my nightmare. Eventually, I'll wake up, and this will all be over."*

Peri closed her eyes for a moment before facing the spirit. "Until you wake up, how about helping me solve your nightmare murder? Think of the mileage you can get from telling this dream to all your golfing and drinking buddies."

Jason's smile at her suggestion turned into a frown. *"I am trying, Peri. Maybe it's part of the nightmare, but I don't remember anything after checking in to my hotel until I woke up here. Well, sort of woke."*

"I know you are. Wait a minute, Jason. You didn't mention a hotel before. Do you remember which one? Room number?"

"What's this?" Theo asked.

Dean, Hannah, and Maralyn stared between her and the spot where Peri could see Jason's spirit. His mouth hung open, but he squinted his eyes.

"Jason just mentioned arriving at his hotel here." Peri felt as if she was vibrating with the excitement she felt. "Before, he couldn't remember arriving in Georgetown. Maybe, given time, he'll remember who killed him."

Theo cocked his head. "It's possible, but do we have the time to wait?"

Peri drew in a breath and released it slowly. "I guess not. It's a start, though."

"Which hotel?" Theo asked.

Jason told her the name and room number.

"The same one I was invited to," Peri told him. "The next room over."

Dean looked back and forth between Theo and Peri. "This situation is bizarre."

Theo nodded. "You can say that again. Everything we learn only seems to lead to more questions. It's been over a week. If the other room was the crime scene, it should have been discovered by now. I think Alton would have let you know if that was the case."

Peri disagreed. "He might tell Jake or you, but he wouldn't tell me."

Theo pulled his phone from his pocket and texted someone. "We'll know shortly."

"Thank you."

"You're welcome." Turning and leaning with his hips against the counter, Theo looked from her to the others and back. "I have to tell you, this is the weirdest murder case I've ever been involved in."

Peri wasn't sure what to make of that remark. She didn't know how long Theo and the others had been investigators, but she thought it was at least two to three years. Perhaps it wasn't long, but they were doing well, which meant they had to have successfully completed a lot of cases. Hearing hers was the weirdest did not comfort her.

"What do we do?" Hannah asked.

Theo stared at Peri, his marine blue eyes never leaving her gaze. "*We* talk to people, and we figure out who lured Peri to the hotel."

"*And who murdered me?*" Jason added.

"And who murdered Jason?" Peri repeated for the non-ghost whisperers in the room.

Theo nodded. "Of course."

Dean stood and walked over to wave his right hand in front of her. Peri watched as it passed through Jason's shade at about chest level. Dean jerked back, his eyes wide. His gaze whipped in her direction as he snapped his mouth shut. Hurrying back to his seat, he dropped onto it before pointing to the seemingly empty spot again. "That area is cold. Like freezer cold, like on those ghost-hunting shows. There really is something there."

Theo looked at her friend. "Did you doubt it?"

Dean shrugged. "I don't—didn't believe in ghosts," he responded, as if wishing he could still deny their existence.

It was an honest answer. Peri thought she knew what Theo was questioning. Though he had never doubted what she saw, there was that moment he wondered if she had killed Jason.

Maralyn crept forward and waved the hand with the bottle of holy water through the space. She shivered. "Did the holy water do anything to it?"

"No, I'm afraid not, Maralyn." Peri shook her head.

Maralyn nodded. "He's not evil then. It would have hurt him if he were evil." She frowned. "Or maybe it needs to touch him." Unscrewing the lid, she poured some in her hand and tossed it at the area where Jason still stood. She looked at Peri. "Anything?"

Peri shook her head again. "Nope. Sorry."

Maralyn put the top back on and put it back in her pocket. "That's good. It means he's not a demon." She went back to the final preparations for supper.

"I need to run by the office. I want to see if I can check up on some things. Will you all be okay?" Theo asked.

Peri blinked. "Sure, we will. We'll look out for each other."

"I don't doubt that, but do you have any weapons?" Theo asked.

"There are two shotguns, a .22 rifle, and a revolver in the closet in my room," Hannah said. "They belonged to my late husband."

"You might want to at least get the revolver out of the closet. Whoever killed Jason isn't in the spirit realm. They're in ours. As much as my mother would probably approve of the crosses and the holy water, even she would want you to have a physical weapon." Theo frowned.

"I know how to shoot," Dean said.

When they all looked at him in surprise (even Jason), he lifted his shoulders. "What? I was born and raised on a bayou in Louisiana. We had snakes and gators, not to mention other critters. I'm rather good, if I do say so myself. Especially with a .22."

"I'll bring it out for you." Hannah headed for her room.

"As long as something is easily accessible at all times." Theo looked at Dean.

"It's close enough. I can't exactly carry it around with me," Dean said.

Theo's look said he didn't see why not.

"We'll be fine," Peri reiterated.

"Okay, I'll check back with you later." He clapped Dean on the shoulder as he passed. "You and Jason keep them safe."

"Will do," Dean promised.

"What does he expect me to do?" Jason groused. *"No one can see me except you, and I can't manipulate so much as a dust bunny."*

"Maybe you'll be able to sense someone coming." Peri didn't want him to feel badly. The poor guy was already dead and literally in limbo.

Jason brightened.

"I can't sense—oh, you're talking to him," Dean whispered, as if someone might overhear them. "We need a subtle signal to let the non-crossed-over folks know when you're not talking to us."

Jason frowned at Dean. *"That sounds like discrimination to me. You'd think someone like him would be more considerate."*

Just like that, Peri remembered another reason she stopped dating the jerk. "What do you mean by that?" She held her palm out toward Dean to let him know she wasn't speaking to him.

Jason waved a hand toward Dean. *"You know. He's one of those froufrou guys. They get discriminated against all the time. I'm just saying it should make him more considerate."*

Peri shook her head. "There was nothing discriminating nor insulting in anything Dean said. Just keep whatever senses you have open so you can try to warn us if trouble is coming."

"*I was just saying.*"

"Well, don't. I don't want to hear it."

"*Fine.*" Crossing his arms over his chest, Jason pouted.

"Jason was being a jerk. Again," Peri explained when she noticed Dean watching her through narrowed eyes.

"I gathered as much. Don't worry. I won't ask. I need a beer. Do you want something?" Dean stood from the table and headed for the fridge.

"No, I'm good. I think I'll just have iced tea with supper." Peri frowned at the wet spot where Theo had checked for blood.

"I'll get it. And for the rest of you, ladies." Someone pounding on the front door cut Dean off from saying anything more. "Jeez, there is the doorbell. Are you expecting a new guest?"

"No." Peri turned toward the foyer. She looked at Maralyn, but she shook her head, too.

"Whoa." Dean caught her arm as she passed the table. "There is a murderer about, and we don't know who's out there. So much for dead-guy letting us know."

Peri paused a moment. "I seriously doubt a murderer is going to knock on the front door."

Dean held firm. "You can't be sure. What if they're waiting for you to open the door so they can shoot you?"

Whoever was at the front door became impatient. They'd also found the doorbell and were simultaneously ringing it while pounding on the door.

Peri frowned up at him until he huffed out a frustrated breath. "Fine. But I'm going with you."

Peri barely turned the knob when the door was shoved open by a statuesque leggy blonde wearing platform espadrilles, skin-tight culottes in a wildflower pattern, and a purple tank top beneath an oversized t-shirt that hung off one shoulder. Once inside, she spun to stare at Peri through red-rimmed, bloodshot blue eyes. Before Peri knew what the woman was about, the woman grabbed her shoulders with pink-coated talons and stared into her eyes from a much too close distance.

"Where's my Jasey? His bitch of a wife came into the office and told me he was dead and that I was fired. He can't be! Jasey was going to leave her and marry meee!" the woman wailed, ending in hiccupping sobs. The fingers digging into Peri's shoulders released. Instead of stepping back and giving Peri her personal space, the unidentified woman draped her arms around Peri's shoulders, leaning over her and sobbing as if her heart were breaking.

It took Dean a couple of seconds to peel the woman off Peri and move her back a few feet before standing slightly between them. "Who the heck are you? And how did you know to come here?" he demanded.

The woman wiped the tears from her face with her fingers. Peri worried she'd poke an eye out with those long fingernails. Of course, the long, false eyelashes she wore probably acted as protection.

"I'm... I'm Bambi. Bambi Booza," she answered in a voice filled with sultry nights.

Peri badly wanted to look at Jason, but she didn't dare. It amazed her that he was being silent.

"I'm Jasey's fiancée. And his secretary. Or I was." Tears once more flooded over her lower eyelids to stream down her cheeks.

"Pardon, but I just want to be clear on your name," Dean said.

"Bambi Booza," the woman replied with a straight face.

Slipping past Dean, Peri took the woman by the elbow and led her into the family room. "Why don't you have a seat? Can I get you something to drink?"

Bambi stood by the couch. "Thanks. Bourbon would be great."

Peri blinked. "Um, I meant tea. Chamomile might help your nerves. I'm afraid I don't have bourbon." She did. But she would not give this woman any.

She was having a terrible time trying to ignore Jason, who was suddenly doing his utmost to get her attention.

Bambi shrugged, her shirt slipping farther down her arm. "If that's all you've got, it's fine, I guess."

Peri passed Dean as she headed for the kitchen. "I'll keep an eye on her. I also texted Theo. He's on his way back."

Peri dropped her head back. "Why did you do that? Are you two dating now?" she whispered. "Bambi isn't a threat. Unless you think she'll smother us in those augmented boobs or stab us with those fingernails."

Dean's brows drew together. "I wish, but it's not me he's interested in. As to the bimbo, just because she's blonde—which I doubt—doesn't mean she's a ditz."

"I know that. It doesn't mean she's a murderer either, though."

Jason shook his head emphatically. *"Bambi wouldn't kill me. She loves me,"* he said smugly.

Peri ignored him. Until he remembered who killed him, she was going to keep an open mind. "Keep an eye on her if it makes you feel better. I'm going to ask Maralyn to make tea."

Hannah came out of her bedroom just then. She carried a rifle and had a revolver tucked in her pants pocket. The handle was clearly visible because her blouse was rucked up over it.

Bambi watched Hannah. She eyed the weapons with more curiosity than concern, which Peri found interesting.

"We've had a problem with snakes," Peri said quickly before Bambi could ask questions. She looked at her grandmother. "This is Jason's secretary, Bambi. Would you mind asking Maralyn to make her some chamomile tea? She's a little upset."

Hannah nodded. "Of course, dear." She passed on through into the kitchen.

"Please, have a seat, Bambi." Peri waved a hand toward the couch.

The woman finally sat on the nearest sofa. She faced the doors to the back porch.

Dean walked around and sat on the opposite couch where he could face her.

Peri knew Theo hadn't had time to get far, but it surprised her just how quickly he came bursting through the front door. She walked forward to meet him in the front hall.

Theo looked her over from head to toe and back. "Are you all right?"

"Of course, I'm all right." Peri cocked her head toward the family room. "Dean overreacted to the unexpected arrival of Jason's secretary-slash-mistress."

Theo looked over her head at the back of Bambi's. "You've got to be kidding me."

"I wish," Peri replied, listening as they heard a whistling noise from the kitchen. "Maralyn is making her some chamomile tea. Would you like some to calm your nerves?"

"What? No." Theo made a face as if she'd offered him liver juice. "How did she find your house?" His gaze once more focused on her guest.

Peri shrugged. "I'm not sure. Dean asked her that, among some other questions. She only answered one or two, and that wasn't one of them. It could have been intentional."

Theo frowned at the back of the woman's head. "What does your ghost buddy say?"

With the water heated, Peri headed for the kitchen to get the tray Maralyn prepared. Theo followed.

"I haven't asked, and I haven't listened to what he's been mumbling except him saying she wouldn't kill him because she loves him. At the moment, he's just standing in front of her, staring."

"Does he look at her like he loves her?" Theo asked.

Peri's gaze flew to Theo's face. "How would I know? That's a judgment call. One of personal perception on the part of the viewer. I'm not comfortable making that call."

Theo turned his gorgeous blue eyes on her, and she nearly lost her train of thought.

"Is he looking at her like he looked at you when you dated?" Theo asked.

"We were in high school. Jason never loved me. If you have to have a description of Jason's expression, I'm leaning toward lust."

Theo grinned; his eyes sparkled with suppressed laughter.

"All you're seeing is the back of Ms. Booza. You'll understand when you see her from the front."

"Booza?" Hannah asked. "Bambi Booza?" The older woman and Maralyn both fought laughter.

"Booza? That's her real name?" Theo looked from one to the other.

Peri just looked at him in response before turning to pick up the small, round tray. "Why don't you come meet her?"

She headed for the living room. Theo followed close behind.

Bambi, who had been staring morosely across the coffee table at a solemn Dean, turned as they entered. Large brown eyes widened at the sight of Theo. Sexual interest flared to life in their depths.

Peri rolled her eyes as she set the tray on the coffee table. "I don't know how you like it. I brought cream and sugar."

Bambi tore her gaze from Theo to look at the tray. "It's hot." She seemed surprised.

"Yes, it's the usual way to serve it. The warmth also helps settle the nerves." Peri saw no indication that Bambi was anything but the stereotypical dumb blonde. Yet something made her suspect it was a well-cultivated act. But did that mean she was capable of murder? Peri didn't know.

"Oh, okay." Bambi picked up the sugar tongs and dropped four cubes into her tea. She then poured cream until the liquid nearly reached the rim of the mug. Stirring vigorously, she sloshed some over the side. It soaked into the napkin Peri had placed beneath it. Picking up the mug, Bambi downed about half of it.

Dean slid down on the opposite couch, making room for Peri. She took the space beside him.

Bambi moved over about an inch, barely leaving room for Theo. However, he elected to sit in one of the two single chairs at the end of the couches—the one nearest Peri.

Bambi looked from Theo to Peri. After a moment, she shrugged slightly. She wasn't as clueless as she had made out.

"Peri, would you listen to me?" Jason stood behind Bambi now, waving his arms like mad. *"I wasn't going to leave Amy for Bambi. I was going to leave Amy for Sheila."*

That surprised Peri so much she blurted out, "Who's Sheila?"

Bambi jerked as if someone had jabbed her with a sharp stick. "Why do you ask about her? Who told you about Sheila? I bet it was Amy. Was it Amy?"

Jason laughed. *"Amy doesn't know about Sheila. She just thinks I'm having an affair with Bambi. That's why I had to keep it up with Bambi. So Amy wouldn't find out about Sheila."*

Peri fought not to roll her eyes. Amy hadn't been the brightest, but still. Peri bet Amy knew exactly what Jason was doing and with whom. And, seriously, great reason for continuing an affair with one woman—to hide the affair with another one.

"Well, did she?" Bambi demanded. She slammed her cup down so hard it surprised Peri it didn't break.

"It doesn't matter who told me the name," Peri said. "Who is she?" There was something going on here. A third woman involved with Jason meant another suspect.

Bambi scooted back. She leaned against the couch and crossed her legs. Her raised foot began bouncing. "Sheila Wright has been throwing herself at Jasey for months. But my Jasey is—was..." she stopped to sniff dramatically a few times... "He was a strong man. I'm sure he never succumbed to her wiles."

Behind Bambi, Jason rolled his eyes. Peri envied him the freedom.

"Ms. Booza, why exactly are you here?" Theo asked.

She blinked her eyes, long lashes fluttering like a drunken butterfly. "When I heard my Jasey died, I just had to see where he'd taken his last breath. I just couldn't believe it. I had to see it to make it real." Fake eyelashes fluttered more, and a fat tear rolled down her cheek.

"How did you know where to come?" Dean asked again.

"I don't remember. I think I read it in the paper." She frowned at Dean, proving to Peri she wasn't as dumb as she wanted them to believe. "What difference does it make? All that matters is that my Jasey is dead!" The last came out in a wail.

"Jason was murdered," Theo stated.

Bambi didn't react. It was as if she hadn't heard him.

"I'm still unclear what you want from me," Peri said, ignoring the tears slowly slipping down the other woman's face.

Bambi impatiently wiped the tears from her eyes. "I wanted to see exactly where he died. I told you already. I don't think I like you. Any of you." She looked at each of them for a few seconds to make sure they got the point. Uncrossing her legs, she jumped to her feet. "I've had enough of your third degree. You don't understand or care how much I'm suffering. I'm leaving."

Peri, Dean, and Theo stood as well. Peri and Theo didn't move, but Dean followed her as she stomped her way to the front door and let herself out.

"*Thank goodness she's gone.*" Jason walked around and sat where Bambi had been. He reached for the mug of tea, frowning when his hand passed through it.

"Isn't she—I mean, wasn't she your secretary?" Peri asked.

Jason shrugged. "*Yes, but Sheila said I needed to fire her. She said I could do better than Bambi. She was right. I'd planned to let her go as soon as I got back. I'm glad Amy fired her.*"

"Did Bambi know you were planning to let her go?" Peri asked.

"*Maybe. I doubt it. I don't know. Since I told her I had something important to discuss with her. She might have figured it out.*" Jason looked sheepish. There was something he wasn't telling her.

"Or she might have thought you were going to ask her to marry you, you dumb jerk. Did Sheila go and speak to Bambi?" Peri ignored his startlement, which was quickly followed by a look of guilt. "If Sheila told Bambi what you really planned, she may have wanted to kill you."

"*Sheila didn't tell her,*" Jason admitted, "*because I told her I had. And I was going to. I really was.*"

"Care to share with those of us who aren't attuned to the astral plane?" Theo asked as he and Dean both sat and looked at her.

"Jason had an affair with Bambi. As you heard, she thought he was going to ask her to marry him." Peri glared at the ghost. "Instead, Jason, who was having an affair with Sheila, the woman he was really planning to divorce his wife over, was told by Sheila to fire Bambi. Which he says he planned to do on his return. Only he told Sheila he already had."

Theo looked in Jason's general direction. "Dude, you are a class A jerk. How many more women were you stepping out with? It's no wonder someone wanted you dead."

Jason glared back at Theo, which did him no good since Theo couldn't see him.

Peri related Jason's response as he gave it. "Jason says he is not a jerk. He only had an affair with Bambi. Then he met Sheila, who he claims is—was—the love of his life. He hadn't totally broken it off with Bambi, though, because he didn't want his wife to find out about Sheila, and, I quote, 'because I wanted to let Bambi down easy.'"

"That is the description of what a jerk does," Dean said.

"You shouldn't be judging me, you sissy boy."

Peri held her hands up toward Jason. "That's enough. You do not get to call my family names."

"Dean's not your family."

Peri took two steps forward until she was right across the coffee table from the spirit. "My family isn't just my blood, Jason. My family is who I choose." She jabbed a finger toward him. "You are only here because we need to discover who murdered you. You better remember that and play nice."

"Why should I? They insulted me."

"No one insulted you. They told you the truth about yourself based on your own actions. Just because you don't enjoy hearing that truth told to you is no reason to take it out on the people stating facts. If you can't deal with it, I can call in an exorcist."

Crossing his arms, Jason sat back.

"Good choice."

"What's he doing now?" Dean asked as Peri resumed her seat.

"Pouting."

Theo shook his head, chuckling.

"What?" Peri asked. Jason had her nerves rattled.

"This is the craziest murder investigation I've ever been in," Theo replied.

"I believe you've mentioned that before. Try discovering you can see and communicate with spirits," Peri said.

Theo grinned. "You're the main reason it's so bizarre."

"Gee, thanks."

"I only meant that we wouldn't know anything about Jason if it weren't for your new ability," Theo explained.

"Are you any closer to figuring out who killed him?" Dean asked.

"As of now, we have three viable suspects. His wife and his two mistresses all have a motive," Theo stated.

"They wouldn't kill me," Jason argued. *"They all loved me. You heard Bambi."*

Peri couldn't believe how obtuse the guy was.

"Whichever one it was, they had to have a male accomplice. Dead weight is heavy. Bambi wouldn't have been able to lift him. Same for Amy. And supposedly, she has witnesses who place her in Texas," Theo continued.

"Sheila's the wildcard," Peri said. "We need to learn more about her. And find out where both she and Bambi were when Jason was murdered."

Theo pulled out his phone. Before he could do anything, it rang. After a moment, he said, "I'm going to put you on speaker. Repeat what you just told me." He set his phone on the coffee table. "Go ahead."

Jake began speaking. "The autopsy results are in. He can't tell me everything because it's an open case, but he did say two things. Jason wasn't killed at Peri's house. The techs noticed the same small amount of blood as you did."

"What else?" Peri asked. It was a relief to know he hadn't died in her home.

"Your knife wasn't the murder weapon, Peri. It was stuck in the same hole the original weapon created," Jake answered.

"Then where was he murdered?" Theo asked.

"I don't believe they know. He didn't say, anyway. At least it moves Peri off the suspect list," Jake said.

More good news as far as Peri was concerned. She had already purchased a new block of knives for the kitchen. If she ever got the others back, she would donate them.

"We were discussing the three most likely suspects. We have a new one, Sheila Wright. Jason was two-timing both his wife and his mistresses. There has to be a male helping whichever one it is. We need to check Bambi out for travel here and find out where Sheila lives. And we need to find a link with a man, either here or in Texas, who is aiding and abetting."

"I'll get on that right now," Dalton, in the room with Jake, spoke up.

"I can see what I can find, too." Peri knew how to research. She did a lot for her genealogy work.

Theo nodded.

"Great, Peri. I can use all the help I can get," Dalton said. "One more thing. The downed CCTV footage is due to the system being hacked. They don't have a separate system to keep it protected."

"Do we know who?" Theo asked.

"Not yet. I'm working on it," Dalton replied.

"What can I do?" Dean asked.

"Keep an eye on Peri. I need to check some things out, and I can't be here all the time. I'm also hoping the detectives will speak with me," Theo said.

"As long as you're back by eight-thirty. I've got to fill in for a friend tonight. I'd stay longer, but there's no one else to cover," Dean said.

"Don't worry, I'll be back in plenty of time." Theo got to his feet. Picking up his phone, he disconnected and stuck it in his pocket. He looked at Peri. "I'll see you around five-thirty or six. You ladies, keep your eyes and ears open. If something is different, let Dean know immediately."

Peri nodded. There wasn't any use telling them they didn't need a babysitter.

When Theo left, Dean grinned at Peri. "He likes you."

She made a face back. "Hush. I've got work to do. Go practice your routine."

CHAPTER SEVEN

Doubting Detective Moore would speak with him, Theo headed for the hotel where everything had started. Most hotel employees weren't paid well. With the right incentive, Theo knew he could get some answers. Whether they would be the answers he needed to crack the case or not remained to be seen.

With his hair slicked back with hair gel, a mustache glued to his upper lip, and contacts turning his blue eyes brown, Theo went to the front desk and requested the same room Jason had booked. He told her he was here on business and that was his lucky room. The receptionist apologized, explaining that the last occupant had trashed the room and it was under repair.

Theo smiled to himself. Of course, the occupant had.

He asked for the room in which they had attacked Peri. The receptionist smiled happily. Theo smiled back. He might get some answers after all.

Accepting the keycard, Theo made his way upstairs. No one guarded the door to Jason's room, though tape sealed it off. The police hadn't released the room, but they didn't appear to be in at the moment—all the better.

Picking the lock, Theo slipped into the room beneath the crime scene tape. He locked the door behind him.

The room showed obvious signs of a CSI visit. Fingerprint dust was all over the place. Theo surveyed the room carefully. There were no signs of blood, nor of any having been cleaned. Hotel rooms were a crime scene tech's nightmare. Even with good cleaning crews, there would be DNA from countless people. Without evidence pinning a connection to Jason, there would be no way to get a warrant for DNA from any of the suspects.

Right now, there are three: Amy Hughes, the widow, and Jason's two lovers, Bambi Booza and Sheila Wright. Plus, the unidentified male Theo was positive was helping one of the women. Unless one of the two women he hadn't met was a bodybuilder, they would have needed a male to move Jason's body from the murder scene to Peri's house.

Where had Jason been murdered?

It was still possible that someone had killed him here, but a stab wound should have left blood. It wasn't as if a person would politely stand over a tarp so someone could do them in and not leave evidence. The murder scene needed to be located.

Just to be thorough, he checked the bathroom. Nothing there. The police would have removed any of Jason's things.

Carefully, going back into the hall, he closed the door, ensuring it was locked.

Using his keycard, he entered the room he'd rented. The room where Peri had been attacked.

For a moment, he stood still and looked at the part of the room he could see. His gaze traveled to the floor. He imagined Peri lying there, unconscious and vulnerable. It made him furious. Someone had set her up. It was only luck on Peri's part that she hadn't been found in the hotel room with Jason's body.

Though Jason had still been alive when she was attacked. That made little sense, either.

Theo had so many questions and so few answers. Whose body had been on the floor? The man helping the killer or the killer himself? There were definitely two since they struck Peri from behind. Where had Jason been at the time? Not dead because he hadn't been deceased long when his body they dropped his body at Peri's house.

But was he supposed to have been dead when Peri arrived? It seemed the original plan was probably to have Peri discover the body and then knock her out long enough for the authorities to be summoned to find her with it. Or had they originally planned to kill Peri, too, but couldn't because they didn't have Jason? Either way, the first plan hadn't worked.

Neither had their second one of dumping Jason at her house. What would their next move be? Theo would bet they weren't done.

He searched the room. Nothing. He hadn't expected to find anything, but one never knew.

Nothing made sense. The man had to have been murdered somewhere since he hadn't been killed at Peri's house—no matter how they'd tried to make it appear. While it was possible that whoever killed him had planned ahead, the stabbing seemed more spur of the moment.

Except for that, the killer had been meticulous. If the murderer used burner phones to communicate, it might be possible to tie them together. If it was a murder-for-hire, and that was the only tie between the killer and one of the women, they might never be able to prove who it was.

Theo looked around once more. He texted Dalton and Peri, asking for photos of three women. Peri didn't have any except for one of Amy from high school. Dalton came through with pictures of all three. With them downloaded to his phone, Theo was ready to leave the room and find some hotel workers to question.

He'd brought nothing with him, so there was nothing to clean up. Since he'd paid for his night with cash, he left the keycard on the nightstand.

Around two hours later, Theo left the hotel. No one recognized any of the women. However, two of the maids remembered seeing a man several times, but they hadn't really paid attention. Theo got what descriptions he could. Because there was no reason for the women to remember, their recollections left a lot to be desired. At least, his theory of a male accomplice seemed to be accurate.

CHAPTER EIGHT

Peri pulled up all the info on Amy Hughes she could find. There wasn't much. If she was on social media, it was under an alias. There were a few newspaper articles where she and Jason were mentioned. The tax records only listed a Lexus in Amy's name. Jason had a Toyota 4-Runner and a sports car in his name, and the house. It was a little odd that the house was only in his name, but not unheard of. Peri had seen it before.

Her phone buzzed. She had a text from Theo requesting photos of the three women. Unfortunately, Peri didn't have any except a high school senior photo of Amy. At least not yet. She told him so and sent the photo of Amy.

Peri switched her online search to Sheila Wright. She was the wild card.

First, Peri searched in Texas, where Jason and Amy lived, but she couldn't find the woman there. Remembering that Amy believed Jason had come to South Carolina to see her, Peri switched her direction. Jason was obviously meeting someone nearby. It wasn't Bambi, so what if it was Sheila? What if he booked the hotel room as a cover?

Testing her theory, Peri checked the county records. It wasn't a complete surprise to discover a Sheila Wright lived in a nearby town. She didn't have her tag number, but Peri knew what car she drove as well as the street address of where she lived. She still didn't have a photo, however.

After more research, she discovered Sheila worked for a local insurance company. Searching the county court records, Peri found two traffic tickets for speeding and a recent divorce—less than three years ago.

"Jason, show yourself. When did you start the affair with Sheila?"

"I'm not hiding."

Peri shook her head. "I didn't say you were. Just show yourself and answer the question."

Jason materialized, sitting in a chair across the desk from her. *"We're not having an affair. Sheila is the love of my life. My soulmate. I know that sounds stupid, but it's true. I met her three years ago at a corporate party. It was kismet. We recognized right away we were meant to be together. Neither of us had ever felt anything like it."*

Peri didn't have the heart to remind him of his recent demise. That answered the divorce question for Sheila. Why hadn't Jason already divorced Amy?

"How long have you known Bambi?"

Jason shrugged. *"About sixteen years, give or take. When my old-in-more-ways-than-one secretary retired, HR sent Bambi to replace her."*

"How long did it take you to start sleeping with her?"

"About a week." He sounded pleased with himself.

"Do I even want to know how many affairs you've had?"

"I don't know. Do you know how many you've had?" Jason grinned, waggling his eyebrows.

"Yuck! I am so glad I broke up with you when I did. You are a jerk, and that's being polite. If Amy is the one who killed you, I'm going to have a difficult time blaming her."

Jason frowned. *"Can I help it if women fall for me?"*

"It was your choice to act on it. It was your choice to betray the vows you took with Amy. That you could have helped, Jason. You could have behaved like an adult. If you no longer loved Amy, you should have just left her." Peri no longer felt sorry for him.

Jason leaned forward, still frowning. *"Don't feel sorry for Amy. She'd had her own affairs over the years. She thought I didn't know about them, but I did."*

Maybe Amy and Jason deserved each other. What a horrible way to live!

Shaking her head, Peri looked back at her computer. It was time to check out Miss Boozer. By the time Theo returned, she planned to have a dossier on each woman. She figured Dalton was already providing him with one, but she might still find something Dalton missed.

By the time Peri finished, her head was aching again. She didn't know how much was leftover from her concussion and how much from dealing with a misogynistic jerk of a spirit.

It was too hot for the screened loggia, even if she turned on the ceiling fans. They weren't expecting any new guests until the next day. Hannah was out with friends, and Maralyn had left for the day. So, Peri opted for the couch in the family room. She put the information she'd collected and printed in a folder on the coffee table in front of her.

After Theo entered Peri's house through the mudroom door, he walked through the kitchen to the family room. He didn't see Peri at first. Dean sat in a chair facing the door. When he saw Theo, he pointed to the couch and then pressed his index finger to his lips.

Theo eased forward until he saw Peri curled up on the couch.

"Is she okay?" Theo mouthed the question.

Dean nodded. "Just too much searching on the computer screen. It may have paid off." He held up the sheets of paper in his hand and used them to point to a folder of more documents on the coffee table. "She left you a present. Though, except for a general resemblance in appearance, Jason's three women are different in lifestyles," he whispered.

Theo took the papers Dean handed him. He picked up the folder containing the rest before sitting in the other chair. First, he looked at the photos of the three women. A couple were better and more recent than those Dalton provided. He looked at Dean. "There are two brunettes and one blonde."

Dean rolled his eyes. "Puhleeze. If Bambi's a natural blonde, I'm a headliner in Vegas."

Theo studied the photos more closely. Bambi did have dark eyebrows. So, three brunettes with similar body types, if not height. Theo frowned. Startled by what he was seeing, he looked at Peri. Were all Jason's lovers replacements for the one woman he couldn't have—Peri?

Theo carefully went through the papers and notes Peri wrote. She uncovered a lot of information. None of which pointed to any one woman as Jason's murderer.

For most murderers, motive often came down to one of three reasons—fear, jealousy, or money. Sometimes, two combined. Rarely all three. Theo didn't see anyone killing Jason out of fear. From what Theo could tell, the guy was a Grade-A jerk, but he wasn't violent or mean. Each woman had a legitimate reason to be jealous. And Amy, at least, had money as a motive. Jason had over eight hundred thousand between the two bank accounts Dalton uncovered. Not to mention his house, his parent's land—which he inherited—two vehicles, and a nice fishing boat.

Jason believed he was well-liked. Theo wasn't so sure. Personally, he found him, just in spirit form, to be an SOB. He would bet money there were others who felt the same about Jason when he was still alive. Right now, they were going on the theory that it was one of the women, but it could just as easily have been an angry business partner. Or a jealous lover of one woman.

Thanks to Dalton and Peri, they had a lot of information. But did they have enough? Did they possess enough knowledge to narrow it down conclusively to one of the three women? Probably not, but they'd just have to begin with the women and work their way out, and they eliminated suspects.

"Did you learn anything at the hotel?" Dean asked.

Theo looked up from the papers. "No one remembers seeing any of the women. Two did remember seeing a man near the two rooms around the time Peri was there. They described him as between five-ten and six feet. Wearing a baseball cap, so they can't give me hair color or describe his face. White, with tanned skin."

"That doesn't sound particularly helpful," Peri said.

"How long have you been awake?" Theo asked.

Peri sat up. "Not long. Enough to hear the last."

"I'd love to stay, but I've got to run if I want to get to work on time." Dean stood. "I ordered pizzas. Willabet said she'd pick them up. She and Kevin should be here any moment." He bolted.

"Willabet and Kevin?" Theo inquired. "Your cousin?"

Peri frowned. "My cousin and best friend, and her husband. How did you know?"

"Jake mentioned Willabet earlier. Your family has some unique names." Theo smiled. Peri laughed, which made him happy. It was the first laugh he'd heard in a while.

"Yes, I guess we do. Maybe that's why Willabet married Kevin. To have a normal name in the family."

Now it was Theo's turn to laugh.

Peri sobered. "Don't mention the hotel, okay? At least not what happened there. They were away on vacation, and I didn't tell them."

Theo nodded. "Sure. No problem."

"Are we any closer to figuring out who murdered Jason?" Peri asked.

"We have more info than before, thanks to you and Dalton, so I will say yes. Are we nearer to narrowing down which of our three primary suspects did the deed? No."

"They did not knife Jason here. It would take a powerful man or two strong women to move him," Peri said.

"I'm leaning toward a man. Jason was a player. We know Bambi and Sheila have no problem going out with a married man. It wouldn't surprise me if they don't have another man in the wings if Jason didn't work out," Theo said.

"Jason wants to know if you're kidding. He thinks you're full of it," Peri relayed the message.

Theo looked to Peri's left. He couldn't see a blasted thing on the couch beside her, yet he knew from watching her that was where she saw him. "No, Jason, I'm not kidding. Do you honestly believe one, or more, of your women wouldn't be two-timing you the way you did them?"

Peri rolled her eyes. "He already knows Amy was. He told me so. As for the other two, he doesn't believe it. They both love him."

Theo snorted. "Just like he loved them. Except if someone truly loves someone, that person doesn't cheat on them." Though, he found it interesting that Amy also had affairs.

Peri turned to her left. "Oh, get real. Do the women know that?" She looked at Theo. "He says they had open relationships and were all okay with that."

"Right," Theo said skeptically.

"I can see two, or even all three, women working together to do him in," Peri said. She frowned at a spot to her left before turning back to smile at Theo.

Theo put the papers back in the folder and dropped in on the table beside him. "We need more information to see if we can narrow it down. Dalton's working on some angles, but if they don't pan out, we're going to have to rethink our next move."

Peri suddenly sat up straight. "Willabet and Kevin are here." She got to her feet, nodding toward the folder. "Hide those in the end table drawer. The less Willabet knows, the better. I don't want her to worry."

While Peri went toward the door to the rear porch to let her cousins in, Theo quickly shoved the folder into the drawer of the nearest end table. He stood just as Peri returned, followed by a woman about five-four with cinnamon hair and brown eyes much like Peri's. She grinned at the sight of him.

Close behind her came her husband, carrying three pizza boxes and a paper sack. He was muscled, around six feet, six feet-one with military-short brown hair and light blue eyes. He smiled, nodding once at Theo as he headed for the breakfast table, where he unloaded his burden.

As soon as Kevin's hands were free, Peri began the introductions. "Theo, my cousin Willabet, and her husband, Kevin Jordan. Willabet, Kevin, this is a friend of mine, Theo Navarro."

The three made the customary greetings to one another, and then Peri got wine glasses and a chilled bottle of red wine from the fridge. Willabet got plates and utensils.

Theo thoroughly enjoyed the evening. They spent a couple of hours slowly eating pizzas and salad and drinking wine. Willabet was funny. She had a ball teasing him and Peri. It brought out a lighthearted side of Peri that he had previously only glimpsed. Kevin was a guy Theo could become friends with. The man was intelligent. He could converse on any number of topics. Peri made a pot of coffee and pulled a strawberry cheesecake from the fridge.

By the time everyone finished and Peri's cousins left, it was after ten-thirty. Theo was tired. His bedroom in the attic was ready for him. They'd moved in the bedroom furniture the previous afternoon. He wasn't prepared to leave Peri yet, either.

Theo also wasn't going to bed until he knew Hannah was safely home.

After he helped Peri clear the dishes from the table, they put them in the dishwasher. While she wiped the table and countertops, Theo carried the trash out to the can beside the garage.

Theo didn't see her when he returned through the mudroom. "Peri?"

"Here." A hand popped up over the back of the couch and waved.

Walking over, he looked down. "Why don't you go to bed? I'll wait up for Hannah and wait until Dean returns."

"You don't have to. I'm fine. Grannah should be home in a few minutes. As for Dean, he won't be home until around two."

Theo frowned. He hadn't realized her tenant would be so late. He should have if he'd thought about it. Dean worked at a nightclub, after all. Walking back to his earlier chair, he sat. "I'm staying. I'll go upstairs when both of them get home."

Peri swung her feet to the floor and sat up. Pressing her lips together, she shook her head. "Fine. I'll go to bed. I'm not going to waste my energy arguing with you. Good night, Theo." She stood just as the landline phone rang.

She grabbed the nearest one, reading the caller I.D. before answering. "Aunt Gerry, what's up?"

Facing the doors to the front porch, Theo saw headlights flash across them. A moment later, he heard a vehicle stop beneath the porte-cochère. Theo frowned. He knew the next guest wasn't due to arrive until the next day, and it wasn't Hannah returning. She would park in the garage. It was late for a visitor.

"Right now?" Peri turned and headed toward the mudroom door.

Theo jumped to his feet and hurried to get ahead of her.

"No, it's fine. We have free rooms. Are you going to stay? Okay. We're coming... A friend of mine who is renting Grannah's attic apartment... Yes, that guy."

Theo was becoming more intrigued by the moment. He got past her and turned on the outdoor lights.

Peri disconnected and hooked the handheld receiver to her pants pocket. "You can open the door. It's my Aunt Gerry and one of her clients."

Not what he expected to hear, but he was going to get to meet the famous Gerry Rutledge. He still stood in front of Peri as he opened the door.

A woman with dark hair twisted up in a bun stood there. She was about Peri's height and slightly less stocky. She was older, but no way was Theo going to hazard a guess. He knew better.

A couple of feet behind and to her left stood a lanky older man, about six feet tall. He had a mustache and shaggy blond hair liberally streaked with white that glinted in the carport light. He looked familiar, but Theo couldn't pin down where he'd seen him.

Nudging Theo to the side, Peri pushed the door open and stepped around him. She and the older woman embraced. "It's so good to see you, Aunt Gerry."

"You, too, sweetie. I didn't mean to be gone so long." After a mutual squeeze, she stepped back. "Peri, let me introduce you to Pauly Rhodes. He needs a place to live for a while."

The older man appeared slightly embarrassed but eager at the same time.

"It's a pleasure to meet you, Mr. Rhodes. You're welcome to stay as long as you want."

"Thank you. That sounds great," he replied. "I'll, of course, pay rent."

Peri smiled. "We can work out the details later. Let me show you the room. You can have the one above my grandmother's. Do you have luggage?"

"Just Pauly, please. Yes, I've got three bags in Gerry's car."

"His drum set will be delivered Saturday," Gerry said.

"If that's okay," Pauly spoke up quickly.

"Sure. That's no problem. If there's not enough room in your room, you can set it up in the game room nearby." Peri stepped away from her aunt. She headed for the car as her aunt pressed a button, and the trunk popped open.

Theo's mind was whirling. As he followed Peri, her aunt, and the older guy to the car, recognition clicked. "You're Pauly Rhodes, the drummer for the rock band Glass Lightning."

Pauly looked at him in surprise. "You look too young to know that."

Theo laughed. "My parents are huge fans. They still play your albums. I grew up listening to you. I wanted to be a drummer when I grew up because of you."

Pauly looked pleased.

"Mr. Rhodes, Aunt Gerry, this is Theo Navarro," Peri made the introductions.

"None of this Mr. Rhodes. I'm just Pauly." He looked Theo up and down. "It looks like you changed career paths."

"I went into the armed forces right out of college. Did an eight-year stint and then started a detective agency with my two best friends."

Pauly nodded. "Thank you for your service."

Theo nodded as he felt his cheeks heat. It still embarrassed him when people thanked him for what he considered his duty and his honor. Reaching the trunk slightly before Pauly, he grabbed the two largest suitcases.

Pauly pulled out the last one. "I would say you found your true calling."

"I think so," Theo agreed as Gerry closed the trunk and they all headed inside.

"Well, I'm certainly glad you did," Gerry spoke up. "Momma is delighted you're renting the attic apartment and looking out for our Peri."

Peri, walking ahead of him, tilted her head back and shook it before looking ahead once more. She opened the door and held it for the rest of them.

Gerry led the way across the kitchen and up the back stairs. Instead of turning toward Peri's office, she turned left and walked around the second-floor rotunda to open a door above Hannah's room. Pauly followed her. Theo followed Pauly.

Gerry opened the door to an enormous bedroom. Straight in front of them was a sitting area with a loveseat, club chair, and two end tables. Near the other end of the room, against the left wall, was a king-sized bed, a luggage bench at its foot. Between two windows that faced the side of the house was another chair and a side table. Just to the right of the entry door was a closet. To the left was an open door to an en suite bathroom.

Walking across the room, Theo set the two suitcases beside the bench.

Pauly followed, gingerly putting his suitcase on the floor. He looked around the pale green painted room. He smiled at Peri. "This is rad. I can't thank you enough."

"You're welcome. I'll leave you to settle in. If you need anything, just press the red button on the house phone," Peri said.

"I'm sure I'll be fine."

"I'm sure you will, too," Gerry agreed. "Sleep well, my friend."

She turned and went back to the hall. Theo followed Gerry and Peri, closing the bedroom door behind him. He followed them back downstairs to the kitchen.

Gerry stopped between the island and the kitchen table. "Theo, I'm delighted to meet you. I'll be staying until Sunday, so I'm sure we'll get to know each other better. I'm going to park the car and bring in my bag."

"It's a pleasure to meet you, too, ma'am," Theo said. "May I help you with your luggage?"

"No thanks. It's just one. I've got it." With that, Gerry went out through the mudroom and moved her car. Moments later, she entered through the family room door carrying one medium-sized suitcase.

After exchanging hugs with Peri, Gerry went up the kitchen stairs.

"Which room is Gerry's?"

Peri turned to face him, crossing her arms. It wasn't as off-putting as she probably hoped. Theo found it adorable and was having a difficult time not giving her a hug himself.

"It's over the family room. Her door is the one beside the attic stairs. Why?"

"I just like to know where everyone is," Theo explained.

"I'm no longer alone in the house, so you can go on up to your apartment."

Theo hesitated.

"There is absolutely no reason to believe I'm in any danger."

Again, possibly valid. If one ignored the dead body dumped in her breakfast room. Theo didn't believe that was a coincidence.

"Maybe. Maybe not. Anyway, I won't get any sleep until Hannah gets home, so I might as well be the one waiting up for her."

"Well, I won't get any either. Which is why I'm waiting," Peri argued.

"Fine. We'll both wait."

CHAPTER NINE

Peri woke up with a headache. Not an auspicious beginning to her day. She couldn't stay in bed until it passed. She had a guest. Plus, if she waited too long, Jason would show up.

After showering and dressing, Peri opened her bedroom door to find Jason leaning against her grandmother's bedroom door.

He straightened when he saw her. *"It's about time. This is boring."*

"Maybe you should try crossing over." Peri strode past him, heading for the kitchen to begin breakfast preparations since Maralyn had the morning off.

"I don't know how. Besides, I'm not ready. Someone murdered me, Peri. Me! You have to figure out who did it."

"It would make things a lot easier if you could just remember who stabbed you."

"Don't you think I've tried?"

Peri supposed he had. "I'm not a detective, Jason. I don't know what I can do."

"Help that new boyfriend of yours. He's a detective."

"Theo is not my boyfriend. He's already trying to figure out who killed you."

"Great. That's great. But you have to help because you're the only one who knows I'm here." Jason sounded desperate.

Peri guessed he was. She couldn't imagine being in his position. It had to be terrifying.

"I'm not going anywhere, Jason. At least not unless someone besides my family and friends realizes I'm talking to a ghost. If that happens, they'll probably have me committed, and we'll both be in trouble."

"I get that."

"I mean, we're going to have to be careful communicating when anyone else is around," Peri added because she was pretty sure Jason *didn't* get it.

She smelled something delicious even before she entered the kitchen. Now she was salivating.

Pauly stood at the stove frying bacon. He looked guilty when he spotted her come out of the hall. "I hope you don't mind. I wanted to thank you for letting me stay here."

Peri smiled. "I don't mind at all. You're welcome here. There's no need to go to all this trouble, though. Usually, we have a cook, but she needed this morning off."

He smiled. "This is no trouble. None at all. I love to cook, and I seldom got the chance while I was on the road with the band. I've been enjoying it since my retirement. Maybe your cook will let me help her once in a while."

Peri didn't know about that, but Maralyn got Sundays and Mondays off. He was welcome to do all the cooking he wanted then. Walking to the island, Peri took a seat. "We can certainly ask her. In the meantime, knock yourself out, Mr. Rhodes."

"None of that Mr. Rhodes stuff. I thought we settled that. I'm just an old drummer. It's just Pauly."

Peri nodded. "Okay, Pauly. I'm Peri."

"This looks delicious," Jason commented, peeking through the oven door. *"I wish I could taste it, but I can't even smell it. Being dead sucks."*

"Only because you're still hanging around here instead of crossing over," Peri said. She froze when Pauly turned from the frying pan.

"What was that? I don't hear as well as I used to," Pauly said.

"Um, I'm glad you decided to hang around here. I'm glad Aunt Gerry brought you here," Peri responded quickly.

"Thank you." Pleased, Pauly turned back to the bacon.

Peri turned her head to glare at Jason.

He took a seat to her right and shrugged.

Dean walked in a few seconds later. "What is that heavenly smell?"

"Good morning to you, too," Peri teased. "You haven't met our new boarder, Pauly Rhodes. Pauly, this is Dean Robillard. He lives in the apartment above the garage."

Dean looked at Pauly as if he was looking at the king of Mardi Gras. "I don't believe it. My entire family listened to your albums while I was growing up. If you don't mind, I'd love to take a selfie with you later. They'll never believe me otherwise."

After a startled moment, Pauly laughed. "Cool. I'd be delighted."

"Theo and his family are fans, too," Peri told Dean.

"I never realized so many of you young folks would have listened to our music," Pauly said. He nodded toward a plate of fried bacon and sausage. "I made plenty for breakfast. I hope you'll join us. Do you often eat breakfast with Peri?"

"I'd love to join you, and yes, I eat with her most mornings. And I promise not to go all fangirl on you." Dean walked around and sat on Peri's right. He shuddered as Jason's spirit passed through him.

Jason glowered as he moved to Peri's left. *"Rude,"* he muttered.

Peri ignored him.

Hannah was the next to arrive. Her momentary surprise at a stranger cooking breakfast gave way to a smile as she sniffed the air. "Good morning."

Peri quickly made the introductions.

A few seconds later, Gerry and Theo came down the kitchen stairs and entered the room.

"Something smells great," Theo stated.

Pauly looked surprised. "Do you stay here, too?"

Theo nodded. "I rented the attic apartment. I'll be moving the rest of my stuff in today. Dean, Peri, and two buddies are helping me."

"I'd be glad to help, too. I'm stronger than I look," Pauly said. He looked at the pan of eggs. "Breakfast is ready. Shall we?"

They moved to the kitchen table to enjoy the repast Pauly had prepared.

When the meal was over, Theo headed to his old place to make sure everything was ready for them to move it.

After cleaning up, Peri headed to her office to get some work done. They weren't supposed to move Theo's remaining items until around eleven.

Learning that Pauly's drums were supposed to arrive the next day, Dean offered to help him arrange the furniture in the bedroom to make space for them.

Hannah and Gerry went out to visit friends. Then they were going to Murrells Inlet to meet one of Gerry's old school chums for a late lunch.

Peri sat at her desk, trying to focus on a new genealogy project while ignoring the spirit sitting across from her.

Jason left her alone for about an hour. *"Are you trying to find my killer?"*

Peri sighed. "I'm working, Jason." She would leave it to him to decide what she meant by that.

"If you don't figure out who did this, I may be stuck here with you forever."

Now, that was a truly horrifying thought. Peri didn't know if it worked that way. She knew Jason didn't either. She would love to deny it, but he was still with her days after his murder. Maybe he was right. The alternative, that solving his murder might do nothing to help Jason cross over, didn't bear thinking about.

"I'm trying, Jason, but I haven't seen you in years. I don't know who either hates you enough or is angry enough with you to kill you. Surely, you can think of someone who fits the bill."

For once, Jason seemed to take her question seriously.

"Do Bambi or Sheila have an ex-boyfriend who might be jealous?" It seemed the most likely motive. At least from what she presently knew. Or, in Sheila's case, perhaps an ex-husband.

Jason shook his head. *"There were men before me, of course. Neither was dating anyone when we hooked up. I have no idea who either were seeing before."*

This was good. Mentally, Jason had finally moved beyond his 'everybody loved me.' "What about Amy? Does she currently have another lover?"

Jason frowned. *"Amy's still in love with me. She fools around, but she wouldn't kill me."*

"Are you telling me you don't think she knows about your mistresses? At least that you were getting it on with your secretary?"

Jason laughed some more. *"You can't be serious. You knew Amy. She's pretty, but she's also dumb as a rock. Unless Bambi blabbed, there is no way Amy knows."*

While Peri wasn't Amy's biggest fan, she had a feeling that Jason's wife wasn't as clueless about his extramarital affairs as he assumed. If she knew, had he done something to push her over the edge?

Love could so easily turn to hate for some people. Tales of relationship murders appeared on the news about monthly, if not weekly, sometimes.

At this point, there were only a few things she knew for sure. Jason's murder was no accident. Several people probably wanted him dead. And any of his lovers were a potential suspect.

The problem was that he could have also angered business partners or others he had done wrong in business dealings.

Still, Peri believed it had something to do with a personal relationship. Most likely, a spouse or lover. Stabbing seemed an intimate way to kill someone. Maybe because one had to be so close to do it. That didn't mean it was a current lover. Not to insult the animal, but Jason had been a hound dog since high school. There was no telling how many women he had in his past.

It was frustrating. Peri didn't know Jason's current life. Or rather, the one he'd just lost. There were too many possibilities, and Peri didn't know how to narrow the list of suspects.

Who was she kidding? She wasn't a detective. The Sheriff's Department was working on it. So were Theo and his partners. They each had more resources at their disposal than she did. She needed to leave it to them.

Jason moved, getting her attention.

She also needed her life back. Which meant she needed Jason's ghost gone. Peri knew that investigative experience or not, she would continue to try to solve his murder.

Unable to think of anything new to go on, Peri eventually focused on her work.

She heard the occasional noise from Pauly's room as Dean helped him prepare a place to set up his drums. Otherwise, it was quiet.

When the front doorbell rang, Peri checked the time on her computer screen. It was nearly ten-thirty. They should have already left for Theo's old apartment.

She headed for the front door as the bell peeled again. What was with all the impatient people lately? She almost reached it when Dean came barreling down the front stairs.

"Don't you dare open that door!" he yelled.

Peri froze. "What is wrong with you?"

Dean frowned at her as he moved between her and the front door. "You don't know who's at the door, and there's a murderer running amuck."

Peri's thoughts went to her favorite Halloween movie, and she barely refrained from chanting, 'Amuck, amuck, amuck.'

Whoever was outside pushed the doorbell and kept their finger on the button.

Dean turned away and opened the door. "May I help you?"

"Who are you? I want to see Peri Manning. Where is she?"

It wasn't a voice Peri expected to hear. Stepping around Dean, she looked at the tall, stacked woman with straight brown hair and brown eyes. Jason's wife had arrived. "Amy."

"I want to speak with you." Amy didn't make it a request.

"Dean, please move and let Amy in."

Dean frowned, but he stepped out of the way.

Peri moved to the side and motioned for Amy to precede her into the house.

Amy marched past her, turning in the middle of the open hall in front of the living room. She faced her. "I never called you."

"So I've been told." Peri still wasn't sure she believed it.

"Why would I ever want to have a reunion with you? We weren't friends in school."

"That's what I wondered when I got the call."

"I don't understand. Why did you agree to go?"

"Because I was raised to be polite," Peri replied. "I figured I would hear whatever you had to say, and that would be the end of it."

Amy looked around before once more focusing on her. "The police said Jason's body was found here."

Peri nodded. She glanced around, but there was no sign of Jason. Instead of Casper, the Friendly Ghost, she had Jason, the Cowardly one.

"Did you kill him?" Amy asked.

"No, I didn't. What possible reason would I have? I haven't seen him since high school graduation."

"He's having... was having an affair. He didn't think I knew. Jason always did underestimate me."

Peri found that to be a chilling remark. "Do you know who it was?"

"I thought it was you."

That surprised Peri. "Me? Why on earth would you think that?"

"Several reasons. I don't think he ever got over you. And whoever Jason was seeing lived around here. He traveled up here every week for the last year or so. It sure wasn't to visit his family. Any he had are long gone."

"And you just assumed he was coming to meet me." Peri still couldn't fathom it.

Amy nodded. "Who else would it be? He didn't care about any of the other women he had sex with. Not even me, apparently."

"Be that as it may, Jason never had sex with me."

Amy huffed out her disbelief at that.

Peri didn't care whether the woman believed her. She would not waste her time trying to convince her. "Why are you here?"

The other woman looked around. She stopped for a moment to gaze at Dean before continuing her scan. Finally, she said, "To see where they found my beloved husband."

Peri pointed to the door to the family room-kitchen. "Right in there by the kitchen table." Whatever Amy really wanted, Peri didn't care. The woman hadn't been in her house for five minutes, and already she wanted her gone.

Amy's expression darkened. "I hope he suffered." Spinning on her heel, she strutted past Dean back out the front door as fast as her four-inch heels would carry her.

As soon as she cleared the threshold, Dean slammed the heavy door in her wake. "That woman is a bi—"

"Don't say it," Peri interrupted.

"Now you know why I didn't come out," Jason said from behind a column separating the hall from the living room.

Dean walked into the living room and dropped into a chair. "I won't say it, but you know it's true. Was that weird or what?"

Moving to sit on the couch facing him, Peri nodded. "Very. She seems to have hated him, so why come to see where he died? She even hoped he suffered. I can't imagine hating someone that much."

"That's because you are a kind, decent person," Dean said.

"She admitted to knowing he was having an affair. That's motive. It may have made her angry enough to either kill him or have him killed."

"I wouldn't put it past her," Dean agreed. "The woman is cold."

Jason nodded. *Thank you, my man. You understand what's going on.*

"Jason agrees with you," Peri told Dean. "Or he's glad you agree with him."

"To be truthful, if my lover were running around on me, I'd be ready to kill him, too. Not that I would, mind you, but I'd feel like it." Dean pulled out his cell and began tapping.

"What are you doing?" Peri asked, though she thought she knew.

Dean glanced up. "I'm letting Theo know why we're going to be late. And I'm telling him about the latest visitor. I told him to let Alton know, too."

"You are not the Pied Piper. You don't have to let everyone know what goes on here every time something happens." Peri frowned.

"That woman may be a murderer, and now she knows part of the layout of the house. So, heck yeah, I needed to tell him."

Peri shook her head.

"Is everything okay?" Pauly asked from the foot of the front staircase.

"Everything is fine. Just a misunderstanding with an old high school classmate."

"No, it's not," Dean said simultaneously.

Pauly looked confused. He had every right to be.

Before Peri could try to explain, Dean began telling him about Jason's murder and everything before and since. Peri couldn't get him to shut up. Not that she minded Pauly knowing. Since he was living there, he probably should. She just didn't want Dean upsetting the older man.

Pauly walked in and sat in a chair. He listened attentively to Dean, asking questions along the way.

When Dean finished, Pauly looked at her with concern. "I'm glad Dean contacted Theo. This is worrying, and I'm sure your man would want to know."

"Oh, Theo's not my man," Peri said quickly. "He's just a friend."

Pauly looked unconvinced. "He should still be made aware since he's trying to help."

Peri couldn't argue with that. "You're right."

"Someone wants to either harm you personally or get you in trouble," Pauly continued. "It's just my opinion, but it seems to me as if someone has it in for you and Jason, and they're trying to work out a way to take you both out. Thankfully, they only managed to get him."

Dean nodded once, his eyes wide. "It does. I hadn't looked at it like that."

Neither had Peri. She didn't enjoy thinking about it now.

Dean began tapping on his phone once more.

Peri didn't even ask. She had no doubt he was contacting Theo with Pauly's theory.

CHAPTER TEN

They finished moving all of Theo's things into the attic apartment Saturday morning.

It was Gerry's last day at home. Since Maralyn needed the day off, Pauly prepared a roast with vegetables for lunch as a farewell. Hannah, Dean, Theo, and Peri joined Gerry and Pauly at the kitchen table for an early lunch. Gerry had to leave right after in order to get to the airport to fly to Atlanta, where she was brokering a deal for a football player.

After lunch, Peri finally had time to visit New Horizons, a local assisted living center and nursing home. She went as often as she could to read to anyone who wanted to listen. The residents had surprisingly eclectic tastes. The last time, they requested Tolkien. They'd finished 'The Hobbit,' 'The Fellowship of the Ring,' and were now on 'The Two Towers.'

Pauly surprised her by asking to accompany her. She was glad to have him. Especially when he proved a hit with several of the men because it turned out he loved to fish and was quite adept at it. While Peri read to her group, Pauly and six older men sat across the large room, telling each other tall fishing tales.

By the time they left, the elderly residents were happy, and she and Pauly both felt good.

E arly Monday morning, Theo left Peri doing research for her newest genealogy client. Hannah and Pauly were puttering around in the kitchen, trying new muffin recipes. Theo couldn't wait until supper when the rest of them would get to taste-test them.

Dean was off work for the day and was watching all of them.

Theo went into the office to catch up on paperwork from earlier cases. He closed one and left it on Linda's desk for her to send out the final report and bill the client on Monday.

Linda Starnes was their first hire and probably the best move they'd made. She was some distant relative of Dalton's. Though Theo never figured out the exact connection. It didn't matter. Theo was just thankful they had her. Besides being a fantastic office manager, she also handled their bookkeeping. Linda was the grease that kept their office running like a fine machine.

Theo returned to his office. He wanted to see if he could come up with any evidence to prove Pauly's idea that Jason and Peri had a common enemy. He looked up from Peri's Junior High School yearbook that Hannah scrounged up for him as Dalton knocked on the open doorjamb before entering. Dalton was also using closed hours to work on cases.

"What are you doing?" Dalton eyed the open book on Theo's desk.

A frustrated breath escaped before Theo said, "Trying to see if something in the yearbook jumps out at me. Pauly theorized that Jason's death and what's happened to Peri are because of a common enemy who was trying to take them both out."

Dalton's brows rose and fell. "It would make sense. That might explain Amy's visit. From what she told Peri, she knew Jason was having an affair. Amy assumed Peri was the other woman. That would make her a common enemy. It's possible Amy wanted to do away with both of them."

"It's plausible, but I'm not ready to settle on Amy just yet," Theo said. "At least not as the sole perpetrator. The attack on Peri involved two people. At least. We know that. Peri would have known if she'd fallen on some type of dummy instead of a real person. That means a male was on the floor when someone else struck her from behind. I want to know who that man is."

"Point taken. There are two other women—"

"That we know of. Not to insult them, but Jason was a player. We can't be positive there aren't more." Theo couldn't yet tell Dalton about Jason's faulty memory. Or anything Jason had contributed. Neither Dalton nor Jake was aware of Peri's new ability. While he trusted both men with his life, and had on several occasions, he didn't feel this was his story to share.

"I've tried to verify that Amy and Bambi were in Texas when Jason was murdered, but I can't," Dalton said. "However, neither can I find evidence of either woman traveling here. If they arrived prior to the murder, they managed to do it under the radar. They could have driven, but that's at least a two-day drive from there to here. Not the case when Bambi showed up afterward. She flew in. I found the flight. I haven't yet checked Amy for her recent visit, but I don't doubt I'll discover her name on an airline passenger list."

"Hold up. You can't prove either woman was in town prior to Jason's death, but neither can you prove they were still in Austin?"

Dalton nodded once. "They attacked peri at the hotel on the fourteenth. We now know that Jason had already checked into the room adjacent to the one where Peri was lured. However, no one discovers Jason's body until the twenty-second. He wasn't murdered on the fourteenth. There is no indication that they killed him more than a few hours prior to Peri discovering his body. And he wasn't frozen."

"Whoa, back up. Where did you get all this?"

Dalton grinned. Linking his fingers, he turned them palms out and stretched them. "I might have managed to get a copy of the police report. I also might have gotten my hands on a copy of his death certificate. While stabbing was the official cause of death, when they checked the bloodwork, they found a high level of a narcotic. Jason couldn't have defended himself if he wanted."

That could explain why the spirit couldn't remember what had happened to him. "Why not just give him an overdose?"

Dalton shrugged. "My guess. Because stabbing is a physical murder. Hands on. They could have kept him alive and drugged until they were ready to implicate Peri."

"Someone, or more than one someone, has gone to a lot of trouble to set her up. It's strengthening my agreement with Pauly that someone wanted to eliminate both of them."

"That puts Amy at the top of the list in my book. As far as we know, she's the only one who knew them both."

"Amy's tall, but no way could she move Jason's body on her own." Something Dalton said earlier and had been niggling at Theo became clear. "I thought Detective Moore cleared Amy."

Dalton snorted. "He may have, but I haven't. He claimed to have found people who said she was in Austin at the time. No one I've spoken with can remember whether or not she was. Whoever he talked with, I haven't found yet." Dalton smiled. "I got an address for Sheila Wright, though."

Theo closed the yearbook with a snap. "Give it to me. I want to see if she'll talk to me."

Dalton grabbed a pen and paper from Theo's desk and jotted it down. "Just be careful. We don't know she's not the murderer."

"Thanks. I will. I'll talk to you later." Address in hand, Theo headed for his car.

Fifteen minutes later, he pulled into the driveway of a modest brick ranch on a shaded residential street with neatly manicured lawns. Sheila Wright's was no exception. Flower beds surrounded two shade trees and bordered the brick walk to her front stoop.

It was four-thirty. Hopefully, she'd run any errands she needed and was home. He wouldn't know until he knocked. She had a garage, and the door was down, so he couldn't see if her vehicle was inside.

Theo walked to the front door and rang the bell.

A few seconds later, a brunette with a curvaceous figure and a sweet face opened the inner door. She looked tired, and her eyes were red-rimmed. The storm door remained closed, and Theo presumed locked. He didn't blame her. Women couldn't be too careful.

"May I help you?" She asked warily.

"My name is Theo Navarro. I'm looking into the death of Jason Hughes. I understand you knew him."

Her eyes welled with tears. She quickly brushed them away. "Yes, I knew him." She quickly composed herself. "I don't understand. Who exactly are you, and why are you looking into Jason's death?"

Pulling out his wallet, Theo extracted a business card and held it up to the door for her to read. "I'm a private investigator. Jason was a friend of my client's. They left his body at her house."

"You mean Periwinkle Manning. I thought she killed him." A look of distrust flashed across her face.

"No, ma'am, Jason was murdered somewhere else, and his body dumped there to frame her. My partners and I are trying to find out who the actual murderer is and see that they are brought to justice. I hoped I could ask you some questions about him."

"Let me simplify things. Jason and I were lovers. We have been for about two and a half years. I know how this sounds, but we were truly soulmates. Jason had seen an attorney about divorce proceedings. He was filing on the grounds of adultery. His. He was leaving Amy so we could get married. We were planning to start a family. Wait there." She walked back into the interior of the house. Moments later, she returned carrying a piece of paper. Unlocking the storm door, she opened it just enough to hold out the document.

Theo took it, careful to move slowly so he wouldn't alarm her. Looking at it, he saw the name of an attorney and law firm and the contact information. He looked at her in surprise.

"That's so you can verify what I've just told you. Killing Jason is the last thing I'd do." She pulled the storm door shut and locked it.

"Did you tell Jason to fire his secretary?"

Sheila nodded. "I did, but he hadn't done it yet. He told me he had, but I know he hadn't. Jason had such a soft heart."

Theo wasn't so sure of that, but he let it pass. Who was he to mess with her memories? "Did Amy know about you and Jason?"

She shrugged. "I don't think so, but I can't swear to it. But Bambi knew. I'm certain of it." She suddenly looked defeated, and years older than the thirty years he knew her to be.

"Ms. Wright, one more question, please."

She frowned, but she didn't shut the door in his face.

"Did Jason stay with you while he was here?"

She nodded. "He always booked a room at the hotel, but he spent most days and the nights with me. The last time I saw him was the twenty-second. He said he had to go to the hotel and see if anyone had left any messages for him. He never returned. Are we done?"

"Yes, ma'am. You've been a big help." He held out the business card he'd shown her. "Just in case you think of anything else."

She hesitated a moment before once more unlocking the door. She plucked the card from his fingers, closed and locked the screen door, and then shut the inner door. Theo heard the deadbolt click into place.

Theo turned and headed back down her walkway. He had a lot to discuss with Peri, Dean, and his partners. He texted them from the car and asked them to meet him at Peri's.

Forty-five minutes later, they met in Theo's attic apartment. Peri and Dean related their encounter with Amy. Afterward, Theo told them of his meeting with Sheila Wright.

They had narrowed it down to two suspects. And they also knew why it had taken days before they were able to murder Jason.

T heo left Peri surrounded by her family. While he felt she would be safe enough, his danger radar was still going off.

Dalton said, "Sheila's info filled in a few of the missing pieces, but we still have no clue where Jason was killed."

He looked up from going over copies of the info Dalton had printed. "How are you doing in discovering the whereabouts of Amy and Bambi during the time frame of Jason's murder?"

"Not well. It's..."

They both looked at the door as they heard Jake striding purposefully down the hall. A moment later, he opened the door without knocking and walked in.

"Have you heard?" Jake asked, standing just inside the door. He appeared shaken.

Theo and Dalton exchanged glances and then shook their heads.

Coming into the room, he sank into the empty chair. "They found Sheila Wright dead this morning."

"What? Murdered?"

"Are you serious?" Theo asked simultaneously. He'd just seen the woman a few days earlier.

"They're not sure. They just found her. When she didn't show up for work for the second day without calling in, and no one could get in touch with her, one of her friends did a wellness check. They found her in bed. They believe she died sometime Sunday night to Monday morning," Jake told them.

"If they don't know how, it means it's not obvious. So, not stabbed, shot, or strangled. And probably not smothered," Dalton said.

"An empty bottle of sleeping pills was discovered on her nightstand. They're assuming a deliberate overdose. They won't know until they get a toxicology report," Jake added.

"I wish I knew what this means for Peri," Theo said.

"It means she's still in danger until we find the killer or killers. Someone drew her into this mess for a reason. And it wasn't a benevolent one," Jake said.

"I still don't get why they brought her in in the first place," Dalton said.

"Payback? Revenge? Jealousy?" Jake suggested. "We won't know until they catch the murderer."

"We need to know where Jason was murdered. Where did his killer get him? We now know it wasn't at Sheila's. Nor was it in the hotel room he'd booked. It makes it seem likely they waited for Jason to make an appearance at the hotel. But if they didn't know about Sheila, who killed her? And why?" Theo looked from one to the other.

"We need to keep an eye on Peri. I didn't like this before, and I hate it now," Jake said.

A chill slithered down Theo's spine. "We need to hurry and figure this out."

Dalton made a face. "You've got one of your feelings again. I was hoping after several days of nothing, we'd avoid that."

"I can't help it. When they come, they come," Theo said with a shrug. He got to his feet. "I'm heading to Frog Knot. I need to tell Peri and the others about Sheila Wright before they hear it somewhere else."

CHAPTER ELEVEN

Peri passed Theo's car as she pulled into the garage. It surprised her to see him back so soon. He joined them for lunch most days, but it was only a little past eleven, and Maralyn didn't serve lunch until noon. Grabbing the prescription she'd picked up at the pharmacy, she hurried into the house. She found Theo sitting in the den with her grandmother, Maralyn, and Pauly.

They were sitting around chatting, but one look at Theo's face had Peri's heart rate rising by the second. "What's wrong? Has something happened?"

Theo looked taken aback by her question. "What makes you ask that?"

"The fact that you're home early, for one. But more, your expression."

Now the others looked at him, trying to see what she saw.

"I just needed a break and thought I'd come early," Theo said.

Peri didn't believe him. Walking over to where Pauly sat, she handed him the sack from the pharmacy.

"Thank you so much for getting this for me." Pauly took it.

"You're welcome." Peri took a chair where she had a clear view of Theo's face. Something was bothering him. She couldn't force it out of him. She was going to have to try to be patient. Difficult for her. "Where's Dean?"

"He's showering," Hannah replied. "Carl couldn't come today, so Dean filled in to mow around the house. He's soaked."

"I brought some tomatoes from my garden this morning, and Pauly made two tomato pies from them. We just took them out of the oven a couple of minutes ago. I, for one, can't wait to try them. Why don't we go ahead and have lunch a little early?" Maralyn said. "Everyone is here. I don't want the pies to cool too much before we eat them. Just let me mix up a quick leafy salad to go with them." Madalyn got up and went to the kitchen.

Tomato pies had been a summer favorite in her family for as long as Peri could remember. Though her mouth watered from the smell, she wasn't sure she would be able to eat any. She was too nervous, waiting for Theo to tell them what was wrong. No matter what he said, something was bothering him.

"I need to wash up," Peri said. "I'll come back and help set the table."

By the time she returned, place settings were already on the table, and her grandmother was putting ice in glasses that Theo then filled with tea. Pauly helped Maralyn fix salad plates for everyone.

Theo and Hannah carried the tea glasses to the table while Peri and Pauly took in the salad plates. Dean arrived in time to help Maralyn bring in the two tomato pies. Then they all sat down to eat.

Peri watched Theo. He took part in conversations, but it was obvious something serious was on his mind. She waited until they finished the lime sorbet before saying, "Spill it, Theo. What's wrong?"

Theo leaned back in his chair. "There's no lead into this. Sheila Wright's body was discovered this morning. They believe she died sometime between Sunday morning and Monday morning. They discovered her when she didn't show up for work on the second day, and a friend did a wellness check."

That wasn't even on Peri's bingo card. Or anyone else's around the table, from the looks on their faces.

Movement behind Theo caught Peri's attention.

Jason stood in the family room, grinning from ear to ear. Peri understood the reason. Right beside him stood the shade of a woman. She matched photos Peri had seen of Sheila Wright. The woman looked as shocked as Peri felt.

If she died twenty-four to forty-eight hours ago, why was she just appearing now?

Sheila clung to Jason's hand as tightly as he clung to hers. Perhaps Sheila was the love of his life. And of his death.

Peri closed her eyes. That's all she needed was a second spirit haunting her.

"Peri, are you okay?" Pauly asked in concern.

Peri opened her eyes. Nope. Sheila was still there. "She's here."

"Who's here?" Pauly asked.

"You're kidding. Seriously?" Theo immediately knew what she meant.

"Sheila Wright," Peri said. "She's standing beside Jason."

"Where am I?" Sheila asked. *"How did I get here?"*

"You're at the B-and-B I run," Peri said. "I guess Jason brought you here. Otherwise, I have no clue. Do you remember what happened to you?" Peri got up and walked over to the translucent couple.

Sheila shook her head.

"What did she say?" Hannah asked.

"She doesn't remember." Peri knew Theo hoped, as she did, that Sheila would remember what happened, and they would be able to expose the killer and put them behind bars.

Sheila looked at Jason and then back at Peri. *"I can see Jason and touch him. I'm dead, too, aren't I?"*

Peri nodded. "They found your body this morning. It's Tuesday. They believe you died sometime between Sunday morning and Monday morning. That's pretty much all we know at the moment."

"Not quite all," Theo spoke up. "They found an empty bottle of sleeping pills by your bed. They're thinking suicide. I'm thinking murder."

"*I don't understand. I don't take sleeping pills. I never have. There are none in my house. Someone gave them to me. Someone murdered me. Why? What did I ever do to anyone?*"

While Peri felt sorry for the woman for having her life snuffed out at her age, she could think of one thing Sheila had done that could cause someone to want her dead. "Perhaps you should have stayed away from Jason."

Sheila's eyes widened. She glanced at her dead lover and then back at Peri. "*But Jason and I love... loved each other. That shouldn't make anyone angry enough to murder me.*"

"Jason's wife and other mistress, or mistresses, might disagree," Peri said.

Jason frantically shook his head.

"*He and Amy were divorcing. Wait, what other mistress? What are you talking about?*" She turned to Jason. "*You don't have a mistress, do you?*"

"*Of course, I don...do.*" Jason's mouth clamped shut, his eyes wide.

"*What?*" Sheila stared at Jason. Her shock was morphing into anger. If he wasn't already dead, the 'if looks could kill' line came to mind.

Jason tried again. "*You're the only one for me.*"

"*So, you don't have a mistress?*" Sheila pushed.

"*Nooo... yes, I do.*" His mouth once more snapped shut. He looked as if he was in pain.

Peri stared at him as something occurred to her. "You can't lie anymore, can you?"

"*I'm not...no, I can't,*" Jason wailed. He looked flabbergasted.

Peri didn't blame him. For him, it had to be a heck of a shock.

"I don't believe this. I was murdered because I fell in love with a two-timing liar." Stepping away from him, Sheila crossed her arms and glared at him. *"Who are—were the other women?"*

Jason must have realized the gig was up because he answered truthfully. *"Just my wife, Amy, and my secretary, Bambi Boo—"*

"Booza! Bambi Booza? The woman I told you to fire because she was too clingy? I guess I know why she was now." Sheila froze. *"That blonde bimbo was at my house last week. She was screaming outside my door, calling me all sorts of names. Now I understand why. I had to call the police to remove her."*

That was a bit of news Theo and his partners would be interested in hearing.

Theo! Peri turned to find five pairs of eyes avidly watching her. She had a lot to tell them. "Jason, why don't you take Sheila into my office and have a friendly chat?"

"Good idea. Come with me, Sheila. I'll explain everything." Jason led his dead lover away.

"Come on. Spill. The suspense is killing us." Dean was nearly bouncing in his chair. "Sorry, poor choice of words."

Peri waved away his apology as she resumed her seat. She quickly related the conversation she'd been a party to.

"That's it then, isn't it?" Dean looked at Theo. "It appears Ms. Booza is the murderer."

Theo frowned in response. Peri could almost see the wheels turning in his handsome head. "Maybe. Dalton hasn't been able to verify Bambi's whereabouts at the time of Jason's murder." He pulled out his cell and called his partner, quickly relating the pertinent details to Dalton. "Peri got a tip from someone about the incident at Ms. Wright's. Maybe verify it with the town cops?"

Theo looked at Peri. "That was close. They don't know about your ability, and I nearly blew it."

Pauly shook his head. "I still find it hard to believe you see dead people."

"Not all dead people. Only Jason. And now Sheila. I was in an accident and hit my head."

"That was no accident," Dean broke in. "Someone lured her to a hotel room and deliberately bashed her over the head. It gave her a concussion. When she found Jason's body, she was able to see his spirit."

"That's terrible. I had no idea. Gerry didn't say anything," Pauly said.

"Aunt Gerry doesn't know about the concussion. Please, don't tell her. Grannah and I decided she has enough to worry about at the moment."

"I won't say a word," Pauly promised.

"Thank you."

Theo put his phone back in his pocket. "Dalton will see what he can find out about the incident at Sheila's house. He'll get back to us as soon as he has any new info."

"Shouldn't we contact the sheriff and let him know?" Peri asked.

"What do we tell him, Peri?" Theo asked. "Unless you want to admit to him you're seeing ghosts. I mean, I'm sure he'll believe you, but he won't be able to use what you tell him without corroboration. Which, at the moment, we don't have."

"But you said Dalton was going to see about getting the police report. Wouldn't that help? At least point the police in the right direction," Peri pressed.

Theo nodded. "It would certainly point Alton that way. But Sheila lived in town. The report would have gone to the city police. We'd have to give Alton a reason to ask about it."

"If Dalton gets a copy, why can't Jake just make sure his uncle gets one?" Dean argued.

"We'll work on it. First, Dalton has to get it. But to accuse Bambi of Jason's murder, we need proof that she was here at the time he died.

If Dalton finds proof, then her rant outside Sheila's house is going to make her look more guilty," Theo said. "That would certainly set Alton on the scent."

Great. Until they heard from Dalton, they were on hold. Peri hoped he came through. She needed it to be over. She tried to remain optimistic about it, but she had enough trouble dealing with one spirit. Peri didn't think she was prepared to deal with two. She wanted to get her life back to normal.

Dean leaned over and kissed Peri on the cheek. "See you all at breakfast. I'll be gone the rest of the day. I promised to help a friend with a new show costume. If you need me, we'll be in my apartment." After carrying his dishes to the sink, he left through the door to the back porch.

Maralyn looked from Peri to Theo. "It's not too hot today. Why don't you two go sit on the loggia?"

Peri shook her head. "I'm sure Theo has to return to work."

"Not right away," Theo said. "I can spare a few minutes to let lunch digest."

"Pauly, Grannah, want to join us?" Peri hoped she didn't sound as desperate as she felt.

"Maybe another time. It's a little too hot for me. Besides, I found a Clive Cussler adventure in the library that I haven't yet read. I can't wait to dive into it." His blue eyes twinkled. He left the table and headed up the kitchen stairs.

Peri looked at Hannah.

"Pauly's right. It's too hot out there for me. Maybe after the sun gets on the west side of the house. You two run along." Hannah smiled.

Theo picked up his dishes, as well as Peri's, and carried them to the sink.

"You didn't have to do that," Maralyn protested.

"My mom would question her worth as a mother if I didn't at least do that." Turning, he looked at Peri.

Giving in, she got up and went out the door, across the back porch, and into the loggia. The fans were already running. Maralyn was right; the temperature wasn't too bad. Primarily because of the lower humidity and not the actual lower air temperatures.

"How are you?" Theo asked, taking a seat near her. "This has to be stressful."

"It is. But I'm okay. As soon as you solve this, I'm hoping Jason *and* Sheila will disappear. Go to the light or go somewhere."

Theo smiled. "Honey, so far, you're the only one solving it. My partners and I are just along for the ride."

"Right." Peri puffed out a laugh, her cheeks heating.

"I'm serious, Peri. Without your connection to the victim—now victims—we wouldn't have half the information we do."

"I wish I couldn't see them. I just want to run the B&B, take care of Grannah and the others, and help people with their family genealogy."

Theo leaned forward, taking her hands in his. "I know. And you will before too much longer. We're close. I can feel it. But that means the person, or persons, responsible are going to become more dangerous. They're going to begin to feel cornered, and when that happens, they often lash out. Until they're caught, I need you to promise me something."

"What?"

Theo squeezed her fingers. "I need you to promise that you won't go anywhere alone until this is resolved. No more trips to town on your own."

"Why would the killer come after me? I wasn't the one having an affair with Jason. Both Amy and Bambi know that."

"Honey, they came after you from day one. I'm not going to bet your life on them stopping now. If Jason had been in his room when you arrived, how do we know they wouldn't have killed you, too?"

Peri shivered. Theo stroked the backs of her hands with his thumbs. Curling her fingers around his, she held on.

A moment later, she gave him a weak smile and shrugged. "I don't have anywhere I need to go, anyway."

Smiling, Theo raised her hands to his lips and kissed the backs. The shiver this time wasn't from fear.

"If you do need to go somewhere, I'd be honored to be your taxi."

Peri could happily lose herself in Theo's gorgeous dark blue eyes. "I may just take you up on that. What's the charge?"

Theo grinned. "No charge. I'm hoping you'll take me up on it." He turned serious once more. "Even here, please stay within earshot if not eyesight of someone at all times."

Peri nodded. "I promise. We're expecting a couple to check in on Thursday and stay until Sunday. Friday, a single woman will be checking in. She'll leave on Monday or Tuesday. So there'll be some extra folks around."

"She doesn't know when she's leaving?"

"She's doing research. It depends on when she's able to get an interview with someone she wants to meet."

"Do you have the names of these people?"

"Yes. Why?" Peri asked, suspicious.

Theo shrugged. "Just thought I'd have Dalton run a background check."

"That won't be necessary. The couple are in their late sixties, and Mrs. Marr is seventy-four. I don't believe they're assassins in disguise."

"Probably not. Just be careful. I've grown attached to you, and I would be very upset if something happened to you." He bounced both her hands up and down. "Besides, you haven't met my parents yet." Leaning forward, he kissed her on the forehead and stood. "I have to return to work. I'll be back for supper. Unless you need me sooner."

"I'll be fine. If it will make you feel better, I'm working on a genealogy project, so I'll be in my office most, if not all, of the afternoon."

"That does make me feel better. Thank you. See you later." Theo smiled at her before walking out of the loggia to the car park.

Peri sat for several minutes, feeling the breeze from the fan on her skin and listening to the birds sing. Several hummingbirds vied for the three feeders hung from shepherd's hooks spaced among the flower garden in the corner of the loggia and back porch. Wind rippled the water of the pool, causing the sun to glint and flash. Since Jason's appearance, Peri hadn't felt like swimming. She didn't like the thought of him watching her—visible or not. Now that he had Sheila, maybe Peri would get in a swim before bed.

She sighed. She'd sent Jason and Sheila to her office to talk it out. Peri wanted to work on the genealogy puzzle she'd started the day before. However, she wasn't in the mood to referee two ghosts who were probably dead because their lousy life choices put them in the crosshairs of a killer.

Still, she'd promised Theo. She would just have to run the ghosts out of her office.

Peri managed to evict the spirits from her office. Since her aunt wasn't home, she sent them to Gerry's room.

Without distraction, she was able to take her client's family back four generations. She found the link there to an early governor of South Carolina. Exactly what the woman wanted. It didn't take her long to write it up in an easy-to-follow format. After preparing the bill, she was done.

Just as she was writing the email letter to send to the lady, her computer calendar dinged with a notice. It reminded her of her cousin Loretta's baby shower on Saturday. Which reminded her she hadn't yet bought a gift. She would have headed to some shops at Pawley's Island, but she hadn't forgotten her promise to Theo.

Not wanting to bother Dean while he was busy, she texted him, asking if he could accompany her the following morning. Several seconds later, a text came back in the affirmative.

CHAPTER TWELVE

When Theo returned to the office, he told his partners of his concerns and the promise he'd elicited from Peri. Though that made them all feel better, it didn't remove her from danger.

"I want to speak with the divorce attorney Jason hired," Theo said. "I want to know if Amy knew he was filing for divorce."

"Motive, if she did. Even if she got alimony, it wouldn't be near what she enjoyed as Jason's wife," Jake said.

Jake would know. At least about divorce and alimony—even if the alimony he'd paid wasn't in Jason's league.

Jake married his high school sweetheart right before the three of them and a fourth friend were sent overseas. It turned out Laura didn't enjoy being married to a soldier. However, she kept Jake dangling right until the day the three friends who'd survived were discharged. Jake arrived home to an empty house save for a letter serving him with divorce papers.

Because she'd never worked a day of her married life, the judge granted alimony. Jake could have fought it. Especially after a couple of their stateside friends told Jake she'd been seeing another man. They even offered to testify on Jake's behalf. But after years of fighting, Jake wanted peace. He agreed to the alimony payments only until Laura remarried—which took her all of five months.

"Maybe you should be the one to talk with the attorney," Theo suggested. "Can you do it over the phone?"

Jake gave him a look of irritation. "I could. But if we want straight answers, it would be better to do it in person. We need to see the face. Surprise attack. However, they may refuse to see me anyway. But I'm counting on him talking once I remind him his client has been murdered."

Theo shook his head. "You already planned to go. Idjit."

Jake laughed at the use of their favorite term. "Something's got to give in this case. I'm flying out at one-forty-five. If there are no delays, I'll get to the law office in Austin before they close. While I'm gone, someone needs to try to speak to Amy and Bambi."

All three agreed that Peri, and perhaps the suspect who wasn't the actual murderer, could be in danger. They made the decision to warn both suspects. That way, they would alert the innocent person while letting the guilty one believe they were not a suspect. The problem was how to tell them. Dalton and Jake elected Theo to deliver the message since he'd met both women and they hadn't.

Dalton tracked down the whereabouts of both women. Amy was staying at a high-end hotel in Georgetown. She was waiting for the authorities to release Jason's body. The strange thing was that Bambi was also hanging around. However, she was staying in a moderate motel off Highway seventeen on the way to Pawleys Island.

Theo went to Bambi's motel first. It did not surprise him to find her there. Where else would she be?

He rapped on the room door with his knuckles. He heard movement, and he thought he heard a male voice, but there was no reply. "Bambi, it's Theo Navarro. You met me at Peri Manning's house. I just need to speak with you for a moment. It won't take long."

There was more movement, and then the door cracked open just far enough for them to see each other. "What do you want?"

"I don't know if you've heard. They found Sheila Wright dead this morning."

"I heard. I guess guilt over Jasey's death finally got to her."

Interesting. How had she heard? As far as Theo knew, it wasn't on the news because there were no outward signs of foul play, and the news hadn't connected her with Jason Hughes. "You think Sheila murdered Jason?" Also, an interesting take.

She nodded, her blonde hair teased out to her shoulders, barely moving due to the amount of hair spray holding it in place. "Who else?"

Who else, indeed? "Just in case Jason's murderer wasn't Sheila, I just wanted to warn you to be extra careful."

A car door slammed, and Bambi jumped. The woman was terrified. That reaction wasn't an act. Since Theo was certain she didn't see ghosts, she was terrified of someone flesh and blood.

"Why haven't you headed back to Texas?" Theo couldn't resist asking.

"I'm waiting on Jasey's body."

"You know they're only going to release it to his wife."

Bambi nodded, her gaze darting around the area behind him. "I know. But I just can't go home until he does."

There was nothing he could say to that. It would be cruel to remind her that Jason had fooled around on her, too. "Take care of yourself." He turned and headed down the balcony for the stairs. Behind him, he heard the door shut.

The next stop was the hotel in Georgetown.

Unfortunately, Amy Hughes wasn't in her room. Not ready to give up, Theo wandered through the lobby and peeked into the restaurant. She wasn't there, either. He finally located her in a booth in the bar. He had the impression she was waiting for someone, but the person hadn't arrived yet. Theo cursed his timing. A few minutes later and, he might have discovered the identity of the mystery male accomplice.

As he approached the booth, Theo made a slow perusal of the area. There were only a few other patrons at the small tables, the few booths, and the bar itself—none of whom he recognized. Theo hoped someone would make an appearance before he finished his conversation.

He stopped beside Amy's booth.

Amy looked up, a welcoming smile on her face. It died a quick death when she saw who it was.

"May I join you for a moment? I promise not to take too much of your time."

She waved a hand toward the opposite bench. "What do you want, Mr. Navarro?"

Theo slid into the seat. "They found Sheila Wright dead this morning." The statement got no reaction.

"That affects me, how?" Picking up her martini glass, she took a sip.

"Someone murdered your husband," Theo stated. "It's possible that same someone killed Sheila. I just wanted to advise you to be careful."

"Is that some sort of threat?"

Theo shook his head. "No, not at all. At least not from me. But someone did kill Jason, and it's probable that the police will learn that someone also killed Sheila. Since we don't know the motive, anyone involved with Jason could be on this person's list."

That got her attention. Amy's eyes widened slightly before she glanced down. When she once more raised her head, she had her emotions back in control. "Thank you for the warning."

Theo waited a moment, but she said nothing else. That was fine with him. It was after six, and if he didn't leave soon, he would be late for supper. Getting to his feet, Theo nodded to her. "Good evening, Mrs. Hughes."

She nodded before turning her attention to her cocktail. She had dismissed him.

Before he left the hotel, Theo made a detour to the men's room. He waited a couple of minutes, glad no one else came in, and then left. He peeked in the bar and checked the booth where Amy had been sitting. Her empty glass was there, but she wasn't.

If she had been meeting someone, she'd no doubt contacted them the moment he left and warned them off. There was no point hanging around.

CHAPTER THIRTEEN

Peri and Dean didn't leave Frog Knot until around one. It took three shops before Peri found the perfect baby shower gift for her cousin. With that taken care of, they stopped at a few more stores before heading to a favorite shop that sold ice cream and frozen treats.

It was still the height of tourist season, as well as being August in South Carolina, so the shop was crowded. Besides wanting something cold and sweet, most people also hunted an air-conditioned spot to escape the heat and humidity.

Refreshed and feeling a tad cooler, they got in Dean's truck and headed home. To get there, they had to drive south, cross both the Waccamaw River and the Great Pee Dee River into Georgetown, and then head back northward along Highway Seven-O-one. People seldom thought about it, but the Grand Strand was an island cut off from the mainland by the Intracoastal Waterway. Between the Myrtle Beach to Conway bridge and the bridge to Georgetown, there was only the Socastee bridge to get anyone across the Waterway.

All of that meant a drive that might have taken five to ten minutes if they could have driven straight west ended up taking around thirty-five to fifty minutes or more, depending on traffic. Still, it was a pleasant drive. The scenery was always lovely, as most of the last leg was sparsely populated. Peri and Dean enjoyed it right up to the second they heard a loud bang. Whatever caused it made Dean lose control of the pickup. He tried to wrestle it to a stop, but in seconds, it hit a soft spot on the right shoulder and flipped onto its side in the ditch.

The side of Peri's head struck the passenger window, and everything went black.

Noises began to penetrate Peri's consciousness. A couple of people were yelling, including Dean.

"Girl, you better open your eyes and let me know you're alive?"

Peri groaned. Her head hurt. There was something wrong. She opened her eyes, but it took several seconds to realize she was on her side, resting on the passenger door of Dean's truck. The side mirror had bent back and broken part of the window, leaving large cracks in the rest. Ahead of her, she saw spidering cracks in the windshield that made it difficult for her to focus on the ditch outside the vehicle.

Thankfully, the ditch was shallow, and they hadn't had rain in days. There was only a bit of water at the very bottom.

"Peri!" Dean shouted, sending a sharp pain shooting through her head. The seatbelt was the only thing keeping him from being on top of her.

She groaned again, squeezing her eyes shut against the late afternoon sun. She held out her left hand. A moment later, Dean caught hold and held on tightly.

"Don't worry," an unfamiliar voice called out. "We've called nine-one-one, and help is on the way. Are either of you hurt?"

"No," Peri said before Dean could answer for her.

"No," Dean added. "Just stuck."

"Just hang tight." The man said, apparently not getting the irony of the statement.

It wasn't long before they heard sirens. Then, tires squealed as the vehicles stopped nearby.

The truck rocked slightly as someone climbed on the driver's side and peered through the window. Before he'd turned the engine off, Dean had rolled down the driver's window. A deputy appeared in the ditch in front of them, looking through the windshield. It surprised Peri to realize it was Jackson. A moment later, he was gone, replaced by a fireman.

The one on top opened the driver's door. "Is anyone hurt?"

"No," Dean replied.

"Ma'am?"

"Just some bruises and cuts. Nothing's broken," Peri said.

"Good. That's good. We'll have you both out of there in a jiffy," the fireman promised.

It wasn't a jiffy to Peri, but with some creative maneuvering and contorting, eventually, she and Dean were both pulled up through the open driver's door and free of his pickup. They were shepherded to a seat on the wide bumper of a rescue squad while the two EMTs checked them out. She looked around but didn't see the deputy. There were a couple of Highway Patrolmen. Maybe Jackson turned it over to them.

"Just so you know, she was unconscious for about a minute," Dean ratted on her.

Peri wasn't going to mention it. She didn't know how long she'd been out, anyway. A penlight suddenly flashed in her eyes. Because it made her head hurt, she closed them.

"Ma'am, I need you to open your eyes so I can finish checking," the young woman helping her said.

"I just have a headache." Peri obediently opened her eyes.

"You've got a nasty knot on the right side of your head where it probably hit the window. I don't see signs of a concussion, but your head is going to be sore for a while. And you're probably going to have a headache the rest of the evening, too." The woman looked at her, studying her closely. "Are you sure you don't want to go to the ER and be checked out?"

"I'm sure. I'm okay."

"If you say so. Let me clean the cuts on the side of your face and on your arm," she said.

Most of the onlookers had left, but Peri heard a car pull to the side of the road behind them, and the door slammed a moment later. Since the back of the ambulance was facing north, she didn't see who it was until Theo rounded the back, his face ashen.

"Are you two okay? What happened?" he asked, his gaze focused on Peri.

"We're fine," Peri said.

"I think the tire blew," Dean said. "I tried to keep control, but the front passenger tire hit a soft spot on the side of the road, and the rest is history."

Theo turned his attention to the two EMTs. "How are they really?"

The male attending to Dean smiled. "They're very well for having the truck flip on its side."

"She's got some cuts and a bump to the side of her head that will need to be watched for a day or so, but she says she's fine otherwise." Peri's EMT was too liberal with her information.

"Don't worry. I know two elderly women who will make sure they both rest for a couple of days." The pickup drew Theo's attention. "I'll be right back." He walked over to join two highway patrolmen looking the truck over and taking measurements of skid marks.

Theo returned just as the EMTs were finishing bandaging and cleaning Dean and Peri's wounds. "I'll give you a ride home. Do you know a service to call to see about your truck?" he asked Dean.

"I've already called a buddy of mine. He'll be here in about twenty minutes, but we don't have to wait on him."

"Good. Let's get you two home before someone tells Hannah they saw Dean's truck on its side." Theo reached out and took hold of Peri's forearm, assisting her in standing. He waited to make sure Dean wasn't having trouble walking before leading Peri to the front passenger seat of his car. As soon as Dean got in, Theo headed the short distance up the road to Frog Knot.

Peri would love to have avoided telling Hannah, Maralyn, and Pauly about the accident. Even though she and Dean came out relatively unscathed, she knew they would think of what-could-have-been and worry for days. It was, however, unavoidable.

Both she and Dean were pushed to opposite ends of the comfy couch in the family room. Then, they were supplied with whatever they wanted. And when supper was ready around seven, they served it to them on trays so they could remain in comfortable seating.

Everyone ended up eating in the family room so they could be together.

As the meal wore on, Peri began to feel the effects of being thrown around. She recognized how lucky she and Dean were not to have been seriously injured.

Maralyn appeared in front of her with a tray containing two glasses of water and two paper cups. She held it out to Peri. "Painkillers. You look like you could use some." As Peri took one of each, the cook turned to Dean. "You look like you could, too."

"Maralyn, you are an angel." Dean took the remaining glass and cup.

"What in the world happened? How did you end up in the ditch?" Hannah asked. She sat in a chair next to Peri. Peri was proud of her grandmother for waiting until they'd finished eating to ask.

Dean shook his head. "I'm not sure. We were driving along when, suddenly, there was a loud bang. I think the tire blew. But I've never had that happen before. I tried to keep control of the truck while also get it to the side of the road. The front right tire hit a hole or a soft spot, and because we hadn't slowed down enough when we hit it, we rolled to the side. We were lucky."

"Thank God." Hannah reached out, and Peri put her hand in her grandmother's. They clung to each other for several seconds, silently celebrating they were still alive. Hannah was one tough lady, and Peri felt she got her strength from her. Hannah squeezed her hand before releasing it. "I know it's early, my darling, but why don't you go on to bed? You, too, Dean. Why don't you sleep in one of the guest rooms tonight?"

"I'll be fine in my apartment, Miz Hannah. Don't worry. I'll keep my cell with me in case I need someone. I think I'm going to head there now. Good night, everyone." Dean got up. He dropped kisses on the tops of Peri's and Hannah's heads and kissed Maralyn on the cheek.

Bed sounded good. If Peri couldn't go to sleep right away, she could always watch TV or listen to music or nature sounds. "I believe I will turn in. I'll see you in the morning," Peri headed to her room, leaving Theo, Hannah, Maralyn, and Pauly sitting in the family room.

CHAPTER FOURTEEN

Theo was grabbing his keys and wallet when he heard someone sprinting up the stairs to his apartment. With a sense of dread, he stepped out of his bedroom into the entry hall just as Dean reached the landing.

"We've got a problem," Dean said without preamble. The man was pale, and Theo didn't believe it was a result of the wreck.

Theo waved a hand toward his living room. "Come in and have a seat."

Once they were seated, Dean didn't wait. "My friend towed my truck in yesterday evening. He was checking it out this morning. He started with the blown tire."

The sense of dread deepened, settling over Theo like a black cloud of noxious smoke.

"It wasn't a blowout," Dean stated.

That wasn't what Theo expected to hear. "What do you mean?"

"Rusty said someone shot the tire out. He found round spots in the rubber. As in, a bullet hit it. That means someone deliberately shot out my tire. And we didn't see another vehicle. We were the only ones on the road."

"They lay in wait for you to come by. They knew you'd come that way." Theo wished there were other routes to Frog Knot, but there was only the two-lane road on the west and the Great Pee Dee River on the east.

Dean nodded. "That's what I think. They were trying to kill Peri."

"How sure is your mechanic? And do you trust him to know what he's talking about?" Theo needed to know.

"Rusty's dad was a master mechanic and taught him everything he knows. Rusty's been working on motors since he was eight. Maybe before. Both he and his dad hunt. He knows what a bullet hole looks like. No matter what it's in. Believe me, he wouldn't make a mistake on something this important."

Dean's confidence was enough for Theo. "What did he do with the tire?"

Dean's brows drew together. "Nothing. It's at his shop."

"Georgetown County?"

"Yeah, why?"

"Because we need to call the authorities and have them pick up that tire. I was hoping we wouldn't have to bring in a third jurisdiction..." Theo shook his head. "Never mind. I need coffee to think clearly in the morning. The wreck happened in Georgetown County, so they should get it, anyway. We need to contact Alton and tell him to have someone pick it up. Maybe his lab can get some evidence from it to help us out. At least the type of bullet."

"Do you want me to call him, or do you want to do it?"

"You call. I'm sure he's aware of the wreck, but he may want to hear the details from you."

Dean pulled his phone from his pocket. Pulling up his contacts list, he called Alton Calhoun.

Theo listened as Dean went over the info about the tire and the wreck the previous evening.

"He's sending a deputy to retrieve all the tire pieces. Alton is also sending a CSI person to look over the truck," Dean said when he hung up. He put his phone in his hip pocket. "What do we do about Peri?"

Theo had been thinking about that while Dean was on the phone. "We tell her what happened to the tire. They're upping their game, and she needs to know. We also need to make sure she's not alone."

"Yeah, well, she wasn't alone when someone shot out my tire," Dean reminded him.

"I don't want to make her a prisoner, even if she'd allow it, but until we catch the person, she is going to be safer if she remains here."

"It might not be as difficult as you think. Peri's basically a homebody. It's one reason she loves running the B&B. She's even hosting her cousin Loretta's baby shower here on Saturday. Crap. She bought the shower gift yesterday. It was in the truck. I'll have to borrow Hannah's car and get it from Fender's."

"Tell me where it is, and I'll stop by and pick it up on my way home for lunch." Then the name clicked. "Fender's. Your friend's name is Rusty Fender?"

Dean laughed. "His dad has a warped sense of humor."

Theo shook his head. "No kidding. Okay, I'll stop and get it. Can you stay here? The more people around Peri, the better."

"Sure. Sounds good to me. I'm not working until Friday and Saturday nights, so I can hang around all day today. Pauly will be glad to help. Maralyn's like a pit bull when someone she cares about is hurt or in danger. I haven't asked because I'm not sure I want to know the answer, but I think some of her Jamaican ancestors practiced vodun. And I'm pretty sure the housekeepers, Alva and Verdita, have Mayan blood. Then there's Miz Hannah... I'd rather face a grizzly bare-handed than that woman angry. Between all of us, we should be able to keep Peri safe."

Theo agreed. "She needs to stay in the house as much as possible. If they're shooting now, outside will be the most dangerous."

"The older couple is supposed to arrive this afternoon. Guests often hang around here the first evening, so Peri will be entertaining them." Dean stood.

Theo got up as well. As he and Dean headed for the stairs, he clapped Dean on the back. "Let's get some breakfast. We'll tell everyone our plan and see if we can get them to agree."

T heo didn't want to leave Peri, but Pauly was no slouch at guarding. And Dean was going to be home all day, too. Theo would have stayed, but he was eager to get to work, tell his partners about the accident that wasn't one, and discuss the meetings with Bambi and Amy. He'd gone over and over them in his head the previous evening, but had been unable to draw any useful conclusions. He hoped the fresh viewpoints of his friends would spot something he'd missed.

There was a lot to discuss. Not least of which would be whatever Jake learned from the attorney.

He found them in Jake's office. They were waiting for him.

"What happened? I don't suppose one confessed," Dalton said.

"No such luck." Theo took the empty seat. "There's something I need to tell you first." Theo related everything he knew about the wreck.

"They're ramping up." Dalton frowned.

"Did you learn anything from Bambi or Amy?" Jake asked.

Theo shook his head. "No, not really. And both were weird. It sounded as if there might have been a man in the room with Bambi, but she didn't open the door wide enough for me to see."

"Television, maybe?" Jake asked.

"No, because after she cracked the door open, nothing. No other sound."

"Maybe the accomplice?" Dalton suggested.

"Maybe. It gets weirder. I found Amy in the hotel bar. She was obviously waiting for someone. Also, she couldn't care less that Sheila was dead and telling her that the woman might have been murdered didn't seem to bother her either."

"Well, it wouldn't, would it? If she was the murderer," Jake said. "She'd know she had nothing to worry about."

Theo nodded. "True enough."

Dalton rested one ankle on his other knee. "It doesn't get us anywhere, however. They're both still suspects."

That was the problem. Theo hadn't found out anything to narrow it to just one of them.

"A car door slammed while I was talking to Bambi, and she jumped a foot. I don't think she was acting," Theo added.

"Peri's in more danger, and we're no closer to solving this," Jake said.

"We're closer. We're down to two instead of three," Dalton reminded them.

"I hope my visiting Sheila didn't lead to her death." Theo hadn't said it out loud before, but he'd certainly been thinking it since learning of her demise.

"Don't go there, dude," Dalton warned. "It won't do any good."

"I agree with Dalton," Jake said. He picked up a piece of paper from his desk and held it out to Theo. "This was in my email this morning."

Theo took it and discovered it was a toxicology report. Sheila had twice the amount of narcotics needed to kill her. His gaze met Jake's. "But does it mean someone murdered her, or she committed suicide?"

"They're still waiting for the autopsy to be completed, but according to Uncle Alton, they're leaning toward foul play. It seems the coroner spotted some bruising around her mouth and nose, leading her to believe they forced the pills down her," Jake said.

"Did any of us really believe it was suicide?" Dalton asked.

Theo looked at Jake.

"Ah, yes, the attorney. Amy knew," Jake informed them. "They served her with divorce papers two days before Jason came to South Carolina. What's more, they hadn't lived together for over three months. While she was gone to visit her mother one weekend, Jason had the locks changed and left all her clothing in boxes in front of the garage. Amy definitely had motive."

Dalton whistled.

Theo frowned. He wished he could get his hands on the spook. Knowing that he and his wife were separated and how acrimonious that separation was is what Theo considered need-to-know information.

"We've got motive, and we've got opportunity," Dalton said. "Amy was here when Jason died. In fact, both she and Bambi arrived the day before someone lured Peri to Jason's hotel. They both arrived within twenty-four hours of his landing. I finally found them on passenger lists after I widened the scope and pushed the time frame back a few days. Once I thought to see when Jason actually arrived, the rest began to fall into place."

"Did Amy and Bambi fly in together? Are they in cahoots? It wouldn't be the first time a wife and mistress joined forces for payback against the dude cheating on both of them." Jake looked at Dalton.

"Not so simple," Dalton replied. "While we may discover they are, in fact, working together, we currently have no evidence of that. Bambi landed at Myrtle Beach about fourteen hours after Jason did. Amy flew into Charleston seven hours after Bambi arrived."

"You said they both flew in after someone notified Amy of the murder." Theo tried to make sense of what seemed like an elaborate shell game.

"They did. Again, separately. Bambi again landed in Myrtle Beach, but this time, Amy landed in Myrtle Beach, too. Not on the same flight. This return was after each had flown back to Austin the afternoon and evening respectively that Jason's body was discovered."

"I'm getting a headache," Jake said.

Dalton grinned. "I can do a chart if it will help. Let me try to break it down for you. At no time did the two women travel together. Nor did they fly into or out of the same local airport, except on this last trip. Then, they both flew here within twenty-four hours of Jason's original arrival. They then flew back to Austin soon after Jason's body was found. Amy returned here a day after notification of her husband's death. Bambi didn't return until the day before she arrived at Peri's. Clear now?"

"Yeah, it went from muddy to tannin water," Jake responded. "I believe we got the main point. They're *probably* not working together. We're back to one being a murderer and the other being an innocent woman. For me, evidence is pointing toward Amy. She's the one with the motive."

Dalton raised his hand. "Hold that thought. It wasn't easy, but I discovered Bambi took out a life insurance policy on Jason for one hundred thousand. Not as much as Amy will get as his widow, but not chump change, either."

"How did Bambi pull that off?" Theo asked.

"Jason agreed. And since she was his executive secretary, his death would have adversely affected her life. I'm sure neither he nor the insurance company expected it to be cashed in for at least forty years."

"We may need to resort to old-fashioned surveillance on these women until one of them does something to prove their guilt," Jake said.

"Maybe we'd also learn who the male accomplice is," Theo agreed. "This isn't a job for the junior brigade, though."

For straightforward stuff, they had three teenagers employed to surveil people for them. For the more dangerous jobs, they had four retired military on the payroll. Luckily for them, two were women.

"Karen and Mary Ella?" Dalton asked.

Theo nodded. "And maybe Hadley to accompany one of them to Amy's hotel. I'm afraid a lone woman might get her antenna up."

"Let me make some calls and set it up for as soon as possible," Jake reached for his desk phone.

"I'm going to get some work done before I leave for lunch. Then, I'm going to head out a little early. I need to stop by the garage and pick up a present Peri left in Dean's truck," Theo told them.

"Don't come back this afternoon. I think we'd all feel better if you stayed with Peri until this is finished," Dalton said. "If you've got more work to do, take your laptop and work from Frog Knot."

"Sounds good to me." Theo left them.

CHAPTER FIFTEEN

It shocked Peri when she woke up and looked at the clock. It was after ten AM. She couldn't remember the last time she'd slept so late. She needed to shower, dress, and get a move on. They had guests scheduled to arrive in a few hours.

Forty-five minutes later, Peri walked into the kitchen. Maralyn was cooking lunch, and Pauly was rolling out pastry dough for something.

Hannah sat on a bar stool, watching them and chatting. "Good morning, poppet. Did you sleep well?" she asked upon seeing Peri.

Peri walked over, kissed her grandmother on the cheek, and sat beside her. "I did. I didn't mean to oversleep, though."

"You needed it," Hannah said.

"Do you want breakfast or just wanna wait for lunch?" Maralyn inquired.

"Just coffee now, and I'll wait for lunch."

Out of the corner of her eye, near the door to the back porch, Peri watched Jason and Sheila materialize. At least they once more held hands and were smiling. Though she would have preferred they cross over.

"How is Dean?" she took the mug of coffee Maralyn handed her and took a sip.

"Except for some aches and pains, he said he's fine," Pauly said. "He's in his apartment talking to his parents. He'll be back before lunch."

Peri was feeling those aches and pains, too. The warm shower had helped loosen some of the stiffness from her joints.

The front doorbell rang, startling them all.

Pauly wiped his hands on a towel and headed through the formal dining room. Peri and Hannah followed him into the front entry hall. When Pauly opened the door, Deputy Jackson stood on the front porch. He smiled at them.

"Deputy Jackson?" Peri stepped up beside Pauly.

"Miz Manning. I hate to interrupt your day, but the sheriff wondered if you had time to come down to the office and talk with him about finding Mr. Hughes' body?"

Peri frowned. "I already told him everything I know."

"Yes, ma'am, but he wants to go over a few points before he releases the body to the family. If something comes up afterward, it will be too late. I can drive you and bring you back as soon as you're done."

"Darling, Theo wants you to stay around the house," Hannah informed her.

"He does?" Peri didn't know that, but Theo had already left for the office by the time she got up, and she hadn't had time for anyone to tell her much.

Her grandmother and Pauly both nodded. Wow, she must have missed the group meeting.

"I don't think he'd mind if Peri came with a law officer, would he?" Ricky Jackson asked.

Ricky had been a year behind Peri in school. She didn't know him that well, but he'd never been in trouble. She still wasn't happy that he'd pushed to get her arrested when Jason's body was discovered, but he was a sheriff's deputy. Maybe that behavior wasn't out of the ordinary.

"Let me get my purse." Peri headed to her bedroom.

When she returned, Hannah was trying to talk Ricky into having the sheriff come to Frog Knot. Peri's grandmother often expected people to come to her instead of vice versa. Peri wasn't sure if it was because of being the only daughter in a family of five siblings or because, as a teacher, she expected it of her students. Every once in a while, she needed a gentle reminder that not everyone was going to bow to her will.

"Grannah, the sheriff is a busy man. I'm sure if he could have come, he would have. I'll be back as soon as I can." Turning to Ricky, she asked, "Are you ready?"

Ricky nodded. He stepped aside to allow Peri to pass him. Then he followed her across the wide porch and down the steps to his car.

Peri realized her mistake when Ricky turned north instead of south at the end of the driveway. Unfortunately, no one at the house would have seen. The driveway was too long, and with the trees and shrubs all leafed out for summer, any possible view was blocked.

"Are we taking the scenic route?" Peri asked lightly, hoping she was wrong. In case she was right, she tried to think of a way to get her cell phone from her purse so she could call a contact without Ricky noticing.

"Give me your bag?" Ricky ordered.

"What bag? I didn't bring a bag," Peri stalled.

"Your purse. Give it to me."

"Why?"

"Give me the purse now!" Ricky obviously had a short patience quota.

Reluctantly, Peri handed it over. She needed to wait and pick her battles.

Ricky snatched the purse from her hand and lowered the driver's side window. As they passed a particularly dense patch of forest, Ricky swerved into the empty oncoming lane and threw the purse out. He swiftly moved back into the correct lane.

Peri didn't see where it landed. She hoped near the road. Brightly colored, it should be easy to spot if it got caught on something. Its discovery would take a lot of luck, but Peri was an optimist. If they went in the direction of the sheriff's office, they'd never spot it. Only if someone came this way did they have a chance of spotting it and knowing the direction Ricky had taken.

At the moment, someone finding her purse was the least of her worries. "Who are you helping, Ricky?"

"Myself."

Peri wasn't sure what he meant by that. "Are you in love with her?"

No reply.

"Where are we going?"

No reply.

Peri frowned, releasing a slow breath. She knew crooks seldom confessed in real life like they did in movies and books, but her curiosity begged to be pacified.

"Is it Amy or Bambi?"

"Just shut up. You'll find out everything you need to know soon enough."

She knew that was true. However, the more she knew, the better her chance to formulate an escape plan.

Peri looked around at her surroundings. Ricky would have to stop at a stop sign before long. When he did, would she be able to release her seatbelt, unlock the door, and jump out before he could stop her? It would be impossible to get out of the seatbelt beforehand because of the car's safety features. She would just have to try it. What's the worst he could do—kill her? She was sure he, or whoever he was helping, planned to do that anyway.

Shortly, the opportunity presented itself. Peri carefully put her left hand near the seatbelt latch and her right arm on the door rest as the vehicle approached a crossroads. Even before Ricky came to a complete stop at the sign, Peri made her move. Caught in the belt and simultaneously trying to unlock the door, she wasn't fast enough.

Ricky punched Peri in her left jaw. Pain exploded in her face, and she lost consciousness.

When Dean walked into the kitchen of the main house, it surprised him that Peri wasn't there. "Don't tell me Peri's still asleep. Has anyone checked on her?"

"Peri got up about thirty minutes ago," Hannah replied. "She just left with Ricky Jackson."

"She what? I thought Theo told her not to leave the grounds."

"Ricky said Alton wanted to talk to her once more before he released Jason's body. We told her what Theo said, but Ricky said she'd be safe with him and he'd bring her back shortly," Hannah said.

That didn't sound right to Dean. Besides feeling that Alton would have called first, he remembered how badly Ricky wanted Peri arrested when the body was discovered. Going with his instincts, he yanked his phone from his back pocket. "I'm calling Theo."

CHAPTER SIXTEEN

Theo walked out of Fender's Garage, the wrapped package in his hand. He was pleased it still looked pretty good, despite being tossed around. Peri would be happy with it.

Getting in his car, he put it on the passenger seat. He had just started the engine when his phone rang. His stomach clenched when it said Dean. It was going to be bad news. He pressed the button to answer the blue tooth phone.

"What's happened?"

"Ricky Jackson just picked Peri up. I've got a bad feeling." Dean went on to tell him all he knew.

Dean wasn't the only one. "Did anyone call Alton and ask him if he'd sent for Peri?" Theo listened as Dean asked the others. He knew what they'd said before Dean replied in the negative. "Have someone call him and find out. If he didn't, tell him what's happened. I'm going to put you on hold while I contact Jake and Dalton."

Theo called Jake. As soon as his friend answered, he said, "Peri's gone. Ricky Jackson picked her up, saying he's going to take her to meet with Alton. We need to know where those women are. One of them is up to their eyeballs in this, and we need to know which one now."

"Hold on. Let me put you with Dalton while I make some calls."

Theo heard Jake yell. A couple of seconds later, Dalton came on the phone. "What do you need us to do?"

"Get up here. If Ricky didn't take Peri to Alton's—and I don't think he did—then we don't know which way he would have gone. They've got at least a five-minute head start. Probably more."

"Okay. Okay, I'm heading out right now. Where are you?"

"Heading south on the highway by Frog Knot. I'm just leaving Rusty's."

"Okay. I'm at my truck. I'll head north. If they are going to the sheriff's, I should meet them."

Theo heard the sounds of Dalton getting in his pickup. A second later, jazz music erupted into the silence. "I'm on my way. I'll call you back if I see them. A sheriff's cruiser should be easy enough to spot."

"Good." Theo hung up with Dalton. "Dean, you there?"

"Yes. Miz Hannah called the sheriff. He knows nothing about it. He didn't ask to see Peri, and the M.E. hasn't released Jason's body yet." Dean lowered his voice. "Miz Hannah is freakin' out. So am I, dude. What can I do?"

"We need a home base, Dean. It's going to have to be you at the moment. Dalton and I are both on the road that runs past Frog Knot. We're headed toward each other. Jake is trying to get eyes on the two women. Borrow Hannah's and Pauly's phones and take them to Peri's office. I don't want you too far from the older folks. I'll give Dalton Pauly's number. Jake already has Miz Hannah's. That way, we can all call at the same time. You can put each phone on Peri's desk on speaker. We should be able to hear each other."

"I can do that." Theo visualized Dean nodding. "What do I tell you know who?"

Theo wanted to assure Hannah that Peri would be fine. That he'd have her home safe and sound before long, but he couldn't. "Tell her we are doing our best to get Peri back safely and quickly."

Something off the left side of the road caught Theo's eye as he sped past. He didn't want to stop and go back, but his Celtic blood screamed at him. Checking the rearview mirror, he hit the brakes, turned the car around, and drove back the way he'd come.

There. He saw it again. A splash of color in a sea of verdant green. Whipping the car around once more, Theo pulled onto the shoulder. Leaving it running, he got out and went to check. It looked like a woman's shoulder bag. The strap had caught on a tree branch, or he wouldn't have seen it. Jumping the ditch, Theo snagged the strap and hurried back to his car.

The moment he touched it, Theo knew, but he opened it and pulled out the wallet, anyway. A quick glance confirmed his fears. He shoved the wallet back in the purse and tossed it on the passenger seat next to the shower present.

"Call Dean," he told the phone.

"Yes. Anything?"

Theo hated to burst his optimistic bubble, but he needed help. "Not of the good kind. I found Peri's purse. Ricky must have thrown it out of the vehicle. Get Jake and Dalton on the other phones."

"Okay. I'm calling them now," Dean said.

"I need to know where this Ricky Jackson lives. Where would he go to ground?" Theo felt desperation clawing at him. He wasn't from this county. He didn't grow up going to school with these people.

"We'll find out," Dean promised. "Their phones are ringing."

A moment later, Theo heard Jake's voice. "What's going on?"

"I need to know everything you know about where Ricky Jackson lives. He's got Peri, and he headed north from Frog Knot."

"I don't know much about him," Jake admitted. "He was younger than me. A year younger than Peri, if I remember. His family, what's left of them, live south of town. I don't know where he lives, but I'll find out. Are we leaving these lines open?"

"Yes. You, Dean, and I are on separate cell phones at Frog Knot. Dean is overseeing it, and he has access to a landline if we need him to contact anyone," Theo said.

"As soon as I get info on Ricky, I'll let you and Dalton know. Then I'm going to leave Linda in charge here and go to Frog Knot with my laptop. I'll let you know as soon as I know something."

Theo began deep breathing exercises. He tried other things he'd learned in the military to calm him. He needed to get back in that mindset. If he weren't calm, he would have trouble thinking clearly.

An approaching truck caught his attention. Theo watched Dalton drive past, slow down, and turn around to pull in behind him. His partner got out and came around to the passenger side. Theo moved the present to the backseat.

As he got in, Dalton picked up the purse. "Peri's?"

Theo nodded. "Her wallet is in it. So is her cell phone. That's what he was probably disposing of by throwing it out."

"How are you?" Dalton placed the purse on the floor.

"Freaked. Trying to get my Zen back, but it's not working."

"It probably won't, either. JoDawn was three hours late coming home one night. I couldn't reach her on her cell. She'd already left work. By the time she got home, I'd nearly lost my mind, envisioning every horrible scenario that could have possibly happened to her. When I saw her, I didn't know whether to shake her or hold her, and thank God she was safe. I settled on the second option. It turned out she'd had a flat and used the last of her cell battery calling roadside assistance. She didn't have a charger with her. First thing I did the next day was get her one of those emergency chargers to keep in her purse. I know this isn't the same, but at the time, I didn't know that." Dalton shook his head. "Women, dude. They get in your heart and your soul before you know it."

Theo stared through the windshield. He wasn't ready to go there yet. Or to admit that he already had. He wasn't sure which.

JoDawn and Dalton had been together for two and a half years and had been married for ten months. They were good together—a true partnership.

"Peri's smart. She'll keep Ricky busy until we arrive."

Theo knew Peri was intelligent. Ricky and whichever woman he worked with were the unknowns in the equation. Theo felt the killings were personal. Theo pressed the button for the phone. "Dean?"

"Yeah."

"I want you to call my office and ask for Linda. Tell her as soon as she and Jake finish their search on Ricky Jackson, I want them to search Amy Hughes."

"You think Amy's the one?" Dalton asked.

"I do. This is personal. Too personal for it to be anyone else. Bambi didn't know Peri before coming here. It's why they tried to set Peri up from the beginning." Theo thought back to his review of the high school yearbook. "Her maiden name is Sellers. See if Jake remembers her parents' names or those of any other family in the area. We need to check property records. Ricky has to be taking Peri somewhere isolated. Somewhere where he won't have to worry about someone coming up on them by accident."

"I'm on it."

With his phone line open and on speaker, he and Dalton listened to Dean's half of the conversation.

"Hey," Jake suddenly came on the line. "Ricky lives in a condo complex. He wouldn't have taken her there. Besides, Uncle Alton already sent a deputy over there to look for him. But I sent Archie over there 'cause he's the closest. I had him talk to the neighbors and show photos of Amy and Bambi. Guess who they recognized?"

"Amy," Dalton said when Theo remained silent.

"How did you know—?" Jake grunted. "Never mind. Theo got one of his feelings, didn't he?"

"Linda's supposed to be researching any real estate owned by Amy or her family, but she may need you to supply her parent's first names," Dalton said.

"We need to check Jason's, too," Jake said.

Theo's blood pulsed faster. "Whoa, I thought Jason didn't have any family left in this area."

"He doesn't, but his dad owned farmland. Jason sold the house and about an acre or two right around it, but he kept the farmland. He gets paid rent for the crops a farmer grows on it," Jake informed them.

"Is there a barn or any type of structure on it?" Theo asked. This was it. He could feel it.

"There's an open barn to store hay and equipment under. If there's anything else, it's too dilapidated to show up on the county records."

"Send us the address. Then call Alton and tell him to get out there. Dalton and I will meet all of you there." Theo turned to Dalton. "Do you want—?"

Dalton waved a hand toward the front of the car. "Just drive. You're wasting time."

It was a testament to his friends' faith in his feelings that neither one asked how he knew or questioned his decision.

CHAPTER SEVENTEEN

T he pain woke Peri. She reached for her face, but something wasn't right. Opening her eyes, she looked at her hands. While she'd been only half conscious, Ricky had handcuffed her wrists. Well, that explained the difficulty of movement. Carefully shifting her hands, Peri touched her left cheek with her fingertips. Pain radiated out, and she quickly dropped her hands.

"You shouldn't have tried to escape," Ricky said.

Perfect abuse speak to shift blame to the victim—the you-made-me-do-it defense. Only Peri wasn't a victim. At least not yet, and she wasn't falling for it. She was also getting tired of being hit on the head.

They were still driving, so she couldn't have been out long. Peri was familiar with nearly every road in the county. She and her friends had driven them enough when they'd first gotten their driver's licenses. There was something familiar about this two-lane. "I know this road."

"Of course you do. It's the road to my family's land," Jason said from the backseat where he sat with Sheila. Peri jumped. She hadn't expected them to be with her. *"Is this the guy who killed me?"*

"I'm not sure yet, but he's definitely part of it." Why not go ahead and converse with the ghost? She didn't care if Ricky thought she was crazy. Maybe it would throw him off guard.

"What? Who are you talking to?" Ricky looked in the rearview mirror.

"Jason."

Ricky cut a frown at her. "Jason's dead."

"Yes. I could hardly talk to him if he was alive, now could I?"

"I'm not falling for your tricks."

Peri shrugged. He might think he wasn't, but Ricky was definitely on edge. Most people in the South were raised on ghost stories. They might claim they didn't believe, but in the hidden recesses of their mind was always that tiny kernel of doubt. Ricky's was surfacing.

Peri didn't look at him. She simply shrugged and smiled.

Jason and Sheila both laughed.

"You've got him nervous now," Sheila said. "He keeps checking the rearview mirror."

Peri's smile widened.

She needed to remain positive. By now, Peri was sure people were looking for her. She just had to stay alive until they could locate her. Piece of cake.

"Don't worry, Peri. We've got your back," Jason said.

"Thank you, Jason. I appreciate that." Jason's words touched Peri. He might be unable to help her physically, but the moral support was surprisingly comforting.

"Shut up!" Ricky's voice wasn't nearly as deep as it should be. Sheila was right. He was getting nervous.

"I wish I could physically touch things," Sheila said. "I'd love to slap him."

So would Peri. She wished Sheila remembered how she had died.

"Sheila, is any of your memory returning?"

"What?" Ricky squeaked. Yep, he was definitely becoming unnerved.

"Oh, did I forget to mention I can also talk to Sheila? She's here, too," Peri said sweetly.

"You're crazy." Ricky sounded more desperate than convinced.

"I'm sorry, Peri, but I still don't remember what happened right before I crossed over," Sheila said.

"But you remember Bambi coming to see you a few days before?" Peri hoped Ricky would take the bait.

"Would you shut up? No one is here but us. You're talking to air. There's no one there!" Ricky was definitely on edge.

"If you say so," Peri said agreeably.

"Yes. Bambi created such a ruckus I had to call the police."

"You don't remember if Bambi came back?" Peri asked.

Ricky's foot pressed harder on the gas pedal.

"Maybe Bambi returned and killed you." Come on, Ricky, Peri thought.

"Ha! Shows how much you and your spooks know." Ricky laughed nervously.

"So, it was Amy." He'd finally fallen for Peri's trap.

Ricky's head whipped in her direction. He looked agitated now. "It doesn't matter. We're almost there."

"He's right. It's the next drive. I don't like this, Peri," Jason said.

Peri didn't like it either. She wasn't dead yet, and she didn't want to become dead.

"What are you going to do?" Sheila sounded worried.

Peri shook her head, wincing when it caused her jaw to ache. She had no clue what she was going to do. How long would it take someone to realize she was gone and begin a search? She wanted to believe they already had, but she had no way of knowing. The fundamental problem, as far as Peri saw it, was in them knowing where to look.

Giving in to fear wouldn't help. She had to trust the sheriff. She had to trust her family and friends. And most importantly, Peri had to trust the faith she was raised to have.

Ricky turned onto a single-lane dirt track that went through a dense wood. It wasn't long before it opened to a cornfield. He turned the vehicle right and followed the lane around the edge of the field.

"He's headed for the storage shed. It's almost at the back of the property. Judd, he's the guy who farms it for me, won't be around for a while. Ricky's using the place because it's out of the way. No one will interrupt him here," Jason said ominously.

"Aren't you just little Mary Sunshine? I preferred it when you were telling me things to encourage me." Turning her head, Peri saw Sheila elbow Jason in the ribs. Apparently, since she was a spirit, too, he felt it because he grunted.

"Hey, I'm just trying to provide information. Information is power," Jason argued.

Simultaneously, Ricky said, "I've never tried to encourage you. You're nuts. Do you know that?"

"You're right, Jason. The more I know, the better." Peri hoped so, anyway.

A moment later, a gigantic metal shelter with open sides came into view. The end she could see was stuffed to the rafters with hay bales.

"Judd stores some of his equipment at the other end," Jason said.

No doubt where Ricky was taking her. Out of sight of the road and with no neighbors near enough to hear any screams for help. Peri had never been a screamer, but she'd always been a fighter. Now was no different. She would use everything at her disposal to stay alive.

Ricky pulled the cruiser around the far end of the shelter. Parking behind it, he turned off the engine and got out. Coming around the back, he opened her door, grabbed her arm, and pulled her out.

Peri went with him. She had to be patient and wait for her moment. As they came around a huge combine, she saw Bambi tied to the tine of some sort of field cultivator. The change in the woman's appearance from their first meeting was marked. Her poofed, sprayed hair now looked like a rat's nest. She was flushed and sweaty from the heat and humidity, and her eyes were red-rimmed from crying. Mascara left tracks down her cheeks.

"What's going on?" Bambi asked, her voice hoarse and scratchy. Probably from screaming. At least she hadn't just given up. She noticed Peri's bound wrists. "What do they want with us?"

"Shut up," Ricky ordered, causing Bambi to flinch. "You'll find out soon enough." He pushed Peri next to the other woman. "Sit down."

Peri sat. She noticed that Bambi's wrists were tied with rope. Once Peri was on the ground, Ricky moved to a nearby support post and grabbed another piece of rope. When he returned, he tied her hands to another tine before un-cuffing her. He didn't even tie them behind her back.

As he put his cuffs away, Peri surreptitiously studied the rope and the equipment he tied it to. The cultivator rested on the dirt floor. The ends of the tines jabbed in the earth. It was too heavy to lift, and she wasn't sure if they could dig into the packed dirt enough to slide the ropes under. There were some rough, rusty edges that she might be able to exploit to cut the rope.

"Don't try anything," Ricky admonished. "I'll be right back."

Peri shook her head at his retreating back. Did he seriously expect her to sit docilely and wait for whatever Amy had planned? It wasn't going to happen.

"Bambi, we need to cut these ropes and get out of here before Amy arrives." Peri began vigorously rubbing her bonds against a corner of the rusty metal.

"Amy? Jason's wife, Amy?" Bambi asked. She did as Peri instructed and began rubbing the rope against the metal tine.

"Yes. She's the one who murdered Jason. She also murdered Sheila Wright."

"And this hick cop is working with her?" Bambi tossed her head in the direction Ricky had disappeared.

"It seems so."

"Why are they doing this?" Bambi asked.

"My guess is revenge for perceived slights."

"I never did anything to Amy," Bambi protested.

Peri stopped scraping the rope to stare at the woman in disbelief. "You had an affair with her husband."

"Yeah, that was bad," Jason said.

Peri turned to glare at the dead idiot just as Sheila slapped the back of his head with the flat of her palm.

"Hey!" Jason protested.

Bambi focused on trying to shred her rope. "Well, yeah, technically. But it was really Jason's fault."

"Hey!" Jason protested again.

"I mean, if he hadn't cheated on his wife, I wouldn't have been able to get involved with him, now, would I?"

Peri had no response to that convoluted bit of logic. It even made a tiny bit of sense. A *tiny* bit. She shook her head. If this kept up, she feared she would end up as nuts as the rest of them.

She just hoped she didn't end up being dead like Jason and Sheila.

"But he was just so adorable. You know?" Bambi looked at her as if expecting agreement.

Sheila sighed. *"I can't argue with that. She's right."*

Peri could very much argue with that, but she wouldn't.

The sound of a vehicle approaching got their attention. They both looked toward the sound, but because of the ceiling-high stacks of hay bales, they couldn't see anything. Then they heard what sounded like another vehicle.

Peri smiled. That wasn't Amy. Or at least, not Amy alone.

Suddenly, they heard someone running toward them over the packed earth. Ricky sped past, heading for the sheriff's department cruiser. Jumping in, he started the engine and hit the gas hard. The vehicle shot off along the back side of the shed, sending dirt flying into the air to linger in a cloud of dust.

"Now what?" Bambi asked nervously.

"I think the cavalry has arrived," Peri replied.

They heard one car come to a stop as others continued. Two cruisers rounded the shed and kept going, following Ricky. Another came around the side and stopped. Car doors began slamming.

Peri wanted to yell, but she wasn't yet confident in who was there.

"Peri!" Theo shouted.

She was so relieved to hear his voice that it took her a second to respond. "Here! Bambi and I are over here."

Seconds later, Theo, Dalton, and a deputy rushed around the combine to stop at the sight of them.

Theo hurried to kneel beside her. Pulling a pocketknife out, he began sawing at her bonds. The blade must have been sharp because it went through the fibers quickly. Then he pulled her into his arms, and Peri went. He was big and strong, and he represented safety.

"Are you hurt?" Theo asked.

"No. I'm fine." Peri pulled back to see the deputy freeing Bambi.

Gentle fingers touched her chin and turned her face to the right. "You don't look fine. You've got one heck of a bruise forming here."

"I can live with a bruise," Peri reminded him.

Theo smiled. "Yes, you can."

"I don't see any signs of Amy," Dalton stated. "They're chasing Ricky down as we speak."

"Amy hadn't shown up yet," Peri told them. "If she was close, she probably saw what was going on and hightailed it out of here."

"The sheriff put out a BOLO for her. And for Ricky's car number," the deputy said. "We'll get them. Should I call an ambulance to have you ladies checked out?"

"No, please. I just want to go home," Peri said.

"I don't want one either," Bambi agreed. "But I don't want to go back to my motel room. Can I come with you?" she asked Peri.

Knowing how frightened the woman was, Peri didn't have the heart to deny her. Besides, they had a spare room. "Sure. We'll help check out of the motel and set you up in one of our rooms. You're lucky we have one free." Peri didn't want Bambi to think she would not be charged. "We'll get your payment info when we get to the house."

Bambi nodded. "Thank you. That'll be great. Only, I don't know where my purse is."

"Did you have it when he grabbed you?" Dalton asked.

Bambi shook her head. "I went to the vending machine at the motel. Oh, I hope it's still in my room."

Dalton looked at Theo. "If the deputy will give me a ride to my truck, I'll go to the motel and check Bambi out and pick up her things."

"I can do that," the deputy agreed. "I need to go to the motel anyway and see if they have CCTV footage. It will help if the abduction is on camera."

Theo helped Peri to her feet. "Come on. Let's get you home." He kept a supportive hand on her elbow as they walked to his car.

Dalton walked with Bambi behind them. He got the details on her room as he did.

Peri gratefully settled into the passenger seat. It surprised her to see her purse on the floor. "You found it."

Theo nodded as he drove toward the road. "That's what let me know Ricky wasn't taking you to the sheriff's department. If I hadn't, I hate to think how long it might have taken us to figure it out and then find you. And your baby shower present is in the backseat."

Peri smiled at him. "Thank you. You are a wonderful man, Theo Navarro."

He smiled at the windshield, hoping she wouldn't notice his sappy expression.

Peri had never been so happy to see the open gates to Frog Knot in her life. She wanted Theo to speed down the live-oak-lined drive but settled for enjoying the view and letting the familiar setting restore some peace to her soul.

Theo pulled into the porte-cochère soon enough. Peri barely had time to release her seatbelt when the mudroom door opened, and people exploded from inside. Dean reached her first. He was pulling her from the car and into a bear hug. He released her when her grandmother shoved one of his arms out of the way. After Hannah finished, Maralyn hugged her and then Pauly. Peri fought tears at the love surrounding her. She truly was home.

"Did they catch them?" Hannah asked.

"They're chasing Ricky. They shouldn't have any trouble getting him," Theo said. "Amy is on the loose. They're looking for her."

Peri's stomach picked that time to growl. She'd forgotten she had missed both breakfast and lunch.

"Child, you come on in, and let's get you something to eat," Maralyn said.

"I'd love that. I really want a shower first. Give me about twenty minutes," Peri said as they entered the kitchen. "Bambi is going to be staying with us for a bit. Dean, can you show her to a free room, please? I'm sure she'd love a shower, too."

"I would. Thank you. But I don't have anything to change into," Bambi said.

"I'll loan you a dress," Peri offered.

Bambi looked her over. "Fine, but it's gonna be *way* too big."

Peri ignored the comment. It wasn't as if she hadn't heard observations about her weight before. Yes, she was overweight, but she wasn't obese. "Think of it as a mumu."

Bambi smiled, seemingly unaware of the daggered stares aimed at her from the other people in the room. "Good idea. Thanks."

"No problem," Peri said with a half-laugh. Clueless seemed to be Bambi's middle name.

"Let me show you where you can stay. I'll bring the dress up in a minute," Dean said darkly.

Bambi looked him over. "Fine. Show me."

"Front bedroom on the south," Hannah stated. She was putting Bambi in the smallest room.

"I'll grab a dress and be right back." Peri hurried into her room and pulled one of her older, loose-fitting dresses from her closet. Taking it with her, she met Dean and Bambi at the foot of the stairs, and passed the dress to Bambi.

"Well, at least it's soft," Bambi said.

"Up those stairs," Dean directed her. Before following, he turned to Peri and mouthed, "I don't like her."

Peri laughed. She didn't either, but they would get rid of her as soon as they could. She imagined the sheriff was going to want to interview them both.

Leaving Dean to deal with her, Peri headed for her room and a shower. If she hadn't washed her hair, it wouldn't have taken so long. But her hair was thick, and washing it and putting conditioner on it usually took a while. Consequently, it took nearly forty-five minutes for her to return to the kitchen. And that was only because she didn't blow it dry.

"How long is that woman going to stay?" her grandmother demanded as soon as Peri took a seat at the bar.

"I imagine she'll be returning to Texas as soon as she can. Unless the sheriff needs her for something after he interviews us. Probably only a day or two," Peri said as Maralyn set a plate in front of her, along with a large glass of iced tea.

"It can't be too soon for me. She 'bout made me lose my religion," Maralyn stated.

Peri understood. If she hadn't been so happy to see Theo and felt so sorry for Bambi, she never would have invited the woman to stay at Frog Knot. She hoped the sheriff would arrive before the evening to interview them. Typically, they would have gone to the sheriff's department, but since neither she nor Bambi were suspects, a deputy would probably come to them. Afterward, she hoped there wouldn't be a reason for Bambi to remain in South Carolina.

Her grandmother, sitting to her left, reached out to tuck Peri's hair behind her ear. "Did Ricky do this to you?"

Peri had forgotten about the bruise. "Yes. I made him mad," she said proudly.

"I'm glad you did. But I'm even more grateful that you're home safe," Hannah said.

"Amen. Praise God. Thank you, Jesus," Maralyn said, pressing her palms together in prayer and looking toward the heavens. A moment later, she looked around at all of them and clapped her hands. "We're gonna have us a celebration tonight."

"That's a marvelous idea," Hannah readily agreed.

"Pauly, I'm gonna need your help," Maralyn said.

"Of course. Anything you need," the drummer agreed. He seemed to enjoy himself helping Maralyn with the cooking and trading recipes.

Peri ate her lunch and let them plan. She knew there was no use trying to stop them.

Hannah left her stool to join Maralyn and Pauly.

Dean came in and took the empty seat. Theo was already sitting on Peri's right. He was tucking into the lunch plate Maralyn had placed before him.

"That woman is a piece of work." Dean grabbed a slice of cucumber from Peri's plate and scarfed it down. "How are you?"

"Grateful. I don't know how I can thank you all." She looked from Dean to Theo.

"You don't need to thank me, Peri. Ever." Theo's gaze was intense as he looked into her eyes.

Peri didn't know how to respond. Was he trying to tell her something, or was she trying to read something into his comment that wasn't there? Still, she reached out and slipped her fingers over his hand.

Theo immediately curled his fingers over hers and gently squeezed.

From her other side, Dean wrapped his arm around her shoulders. "Hon, you're my family. I'd do anything for you."

Peri fought tears. She leaned into Dean, closing her eyes for a moment and resting her head on his shoulder.

Maralyn leaned over the island, getting their attention. She smiled from ear to ear. "I hate to break this up, but we need a few things from the grocery and the market." She held out a piece of paper.

Dean took it with his left hand. "I'll get... I just remembered. I don't have a vehicle." He stood, dropping a kiss on the top of Peri's head as he released her.

"Take mine. I'm not going anywhere." Pulling his keys from his pocket, Theo tossed them in the air.

Catching them one-handed, Dean headed out.

CHAPTER EIGHTEEN

Theo reclined on a chaise in the screened loggia. He was exhausted, but he couldn't sleep. It wasn't just that the day had been hectic and stressful. His current problem lay in the feeling that the other shoe was about to drop.

He wished Bambi was staying anywhere except Frog Knot. She might also be a victim of Amy's machinations, but he didn't trust her.

At least Alton had finished with her. He'd arrived around four with a deputy and taken separate statements from both Peri and Bambi. Afterward, he'd not only released Bambi but also bluntly suggested that she return to Texas as soon as possible.

The best news they'd gotten was when Alton received a call as he was leaving. His office informed him that Ricky Jackson had been apprehended and was sitting in a jail cell.

Maralyn, Pauly, and Hannah had pulled off a spectacular dinner celebration. Settling on seven o'clock, they held it in the main dining room to accommodate everyone invited. Besides the regular household members, Alton and his wife, Dalton and JoDawn, and Jake were also included. The elderly couple who'd arrived that afternoon were invited and accepted—even though they had no clue what they were celebrating.

No one missed Bambi. Even though she now possessed all her belongings, she elected to stay in her room and have a meal brought up to her.

It would have been the perfect ending to the day if only they'd found Amy. The woman had disappeared. And, lovesick sap that he was, Ricky wasn't talking.

Because Amy was in the wind, Theo couldn't go to bed. The people of this home weren't used to violence. Plus, they welcomed strangers into their home all the time. The gigantic house had too many points of entry to be anything but a defender's nightmare. As soon as he was able, Theo planned to see about getting a security, or at least monitoring, system installed.

Until he could set up some electronic protections, Theo had enlisted Dean and Pauly to help him keep an eye out. Dean had been a part of the family for years. And though the retired drummer had only lived there a week, they already accepted him as one of their own.

Theo smiled in the deep shadows of the loggia. They also accepted him with open arms. No questions asked. Which made him question their judgment a bit.

His mother and Hannah had become phone friends, talking every other day or so. Theo wasn't about to ask about the topics. And his father, a huge fan of Glass Lightning, had become friends with Pauly. All of them, Theo included, were looking forward to his parent's visit as soon as they were able to come.

Movement in the dim lights surrounding the pool walkway caught his attention. Remaining still, he waited. A fat raccoon waddled onto the cement pool surround near the shallow end. It headed toward the loggia steps, followed a moment later by three smaller ones. A cute little family.

As long as they weren't rabid. Theo warned them of the concern, but Maralyn and Peri often left vegetable food scraps near the pond on the property. It was located near the old family cemetery about five hundred yards from the house. Coons and possums often made their way to the house looking for more goodies. Theo had even seen a fox. And, of course, deer.

All the visitors sent Hannah's dog, Jigger, into peals of excited barking every time they released her into the large, fenced yard surrounding the pool. Jigger would search every nook and cranny of the area. Though the small dog never found one of the furry nocturnal visitors, she was happy chasing lizards, birds, and squirrels.

After searching, but finding nothing of interest, momma coon and her young ones turned and headed back off across the lawn. Off in the distance, Theo heard the soft roar of an alligator bellowing. Since the breeding season was over, it was probably just protecting its territory. An owl called nearer to where he sat.

A noise from the house drew Theo's attention. A moment later, a thin shadow came out the kitchen door and entered the loggia. He recognized Pauly. "What are you doing up?"

"I couldn't sleep. I made some coffee and brought us each a cup." He handed Theo a mug of steaming liquid. "You've been up for a long time. I figured you could use some caffeine."

Theo accepted the mug gratefully. "Thank you. I can. It's so peaceful out here it's difficult to stay awake."

"Do you think Amy is going to hang around?" Pauly took a seat to Theo's right.

Theo nodded. "I don't think she's finished. If Bambi goes home, it may make it harder on her. If she stays, then both women that Amy seems to want dead are right here in one place."

"I heard Peri telling Hannah that Bambi has made no reservations to leave yet. They were both hoping she'd find a flight out tomorrow. That doesn't seem likely."

"I've got to tell you, Pauly, I don't trust Bambi."

Pauly nodded. "Any woman that has an affair with another woman's husband isn't very trustworthy, in my opinion. Whether that translates to being a murderer..." He shook his head. "... I just don't know."

Theo nodded. "Me either."

They sat silently for a few minutes before Pauly asked, "Do you think Amy will try to get Peri again?"

"I'd love to say we have scared her off, but I don't believe it. I think she'll try again. Anger is her guiding force right now. Even though Peri is the only one of the three other women who never had an affair with Jason, she was his first love. Look at the physiognomy of Amy, Bambi, and Sheila. Their body shapes all resemble Peri's high school photos. I think Amy has always been jealous of Peri, and I think she knows she was second choice because Jason couldn't have Peri."

Pauly was quiet for a few moments. "I saw Peri's senior photo on the mantel in the family room. You're right."

"I won't feel at ease until Amy is behind bars with Ricky."

"I thought about telling you to go to bed, that I'd stay up and let you know if anything happened, but I can see that wouldn't work," Pauly said.

Theo chuckled. "I appreciate the offer. But, no, it wouldn't. I wouldn't be able to get any rest. However, I might doze off here. It's too darned peaceful. If I do, I'd appreciate it if you wake me."

"I can do that."

Theo didn't know when he fell asleep, but he woke at the sound of Maralyn's car pulling up in the parking lot. Looking to his right, he found Pauly watching him, an indulgent smile on his weathered face.

"Before you ask, all had been quiet. I thought you could use the rest. It seems I was right. You look much better," Pauly said.

"Thank you. I did need it. I have to be on top of my game. Dragging around half asleep won't help anyone." Getting to his feet, Theo stretched. "If you don't mind continuing to handle the situation, I'm going for a walk to see if I can clear the remaining cobwebs."

"Go ahead. Enjoy yourself. I'll go in and see if I can help Maralyn with breakfast. If I sit at the table, I can see straight across to Peri's and Hannah's bedroom doors. You take as long as you need." Pauly got up.

As the older man headed for the kitchen, Theo left the loggia through the door to the backyard. Walking across the pool patio, he followed the cement sidewalk. Once he passed through the side gate, it turned into an oyster shell path. This path wound through ancient live oaks dripping with Spanish moss. Very early in the morning, the sun barely lightened the eastern sky, but it was enough to allow him to see where he walked.

Before long, he came to a narrow Y in the path. To the left, it went toward the pond. To the right, it went to a family cemetery begun four years after the original house was built. The first grave was that of one of the children the original family lost to illness. That child would soon be followed by two more.

Though he'd been that way before, Theo felt drawn to the cemetery. He followed the path to the right. He'd walked past it before (the trail continued and curved around to come back by the pond), but he'd never entered the gates. Theo only read the stones he could see from outside the fence. He knew many of Peri's recent family were buried inside. Including her grandfather, her parents, and her brother. Someday, he would enter and visit those graves, but not today.

Today, Theo needed to return to the house, shower, and check in with Jake. His friend was monitoring the search for Amy Hughes. Theo hoped Jake had some good news. He was getting antsy. It felt like the calm before the storm.

Turning, he headed back.

CHAPTER NINETEEN

Peri finally gave up. She'd managed to get some sleep, but she kept waking all during the night. Every time she did, it took longer and longer to fall asleep again. When she woke a little before seven, Peri decided to go ahead and get up.

Showered and dressed, she headed for the kitchen, only to stop when she saw Jason and Sheila sitting on a couch in the living room, the fingers of their hands linked.

"Oh, dear, you don't look like you slept well," Sheila observed.

"Not well, no. How about you? How are you doing?"

"Well, we don't need to sleep anymore," Sheila said.

Peri took a seat across the coffee table from them. "Now that we know it was Amy who murdered you, are any of your memories of the event returning?"

Jason shook his head. *"I still can't believe Amy murdered me."*

"I don't even remember ever meeting Amy," Sheila said. *"We're so glad she didn't get you, too."*

Jason nodded.

Sheila waved a hand toward the kitchen. *"Go ahead and get your breakfast. Don't worry about us. We'll just wander around the grounds. If you need us, just think about us, and we'll come."*

Peri nodded. She didn't know how to respond otherwise. She had no clue what spirits who hadn't crossed over did. How sad if they just endlessly wandered. It didn't feel right to suggest they enjoy themselves. Standing, Peri simply smiled at them before heading into the kitchen.

Frog Knot's guests, Roger and Clara Cline, were already at the kitchen table with Theo, Dean, and Pauly. Hannah wasn't up yet. Peri had the feeling Bambi was a late riser when she could get away with it.

"Have a seat, suga'. Whatcha want for breakfast?" Maralyn asked as Peri got a mug and filled it with hot coffee.

"Eggs, bacon, and toast, please." She didn't have to ask for butter. Everyone in the family knew she loved butter. Peri joined the others at the table. She exchanged greetings as she added cream to her coffee. Needing at least half a cup to be fully sociable, she listened to the conversation flow around her.

Peri nearly finished eating when the tippity-tap of doggy toenails heralded Jigger's arrival. Hannah followed behind.

By the time her grandmother finished, the Clines had asked her and the others multiple questions about local sites and were eager to be off to explore Georgetown and northward along the coast toward Myrtle Beach. After a quick visit to their room to gather what they needed, they were off.

"Any signs of movement from Bambi?" Hannah asked.

"Nothin'," Maralyn said with a frown. "You don' s'pose she's plannin' to camp out up there, do ya?"

"If she is, she's going to need an alternate way to get food and water, because there will be no more deliveries to her room," Hannah declared.

"I just hope she arranges to return to Texas tomorrow. I think it's probably too late for her to get a flight out today," Peri said.

"If she doesn't leave tomorrow, I'll have no problem throwing her out for you," Dean offered.

Peri wanted the woman gone, too, but still. "I hope it doesn't come to that. I'll talk to her when she comes down."

"If she comes down," Maralyn muttered as she joined them at the table.

"What are all your plans for today?" Theo asked. He looked at Dean first.

"Just hanging around here until around four-thirty. Then I'm heading to work. I should be back around two," Dean replied.

Pauly was next.

"When I'm not helping Maralyn, I'll be on the patio reading the Clive Cussler book I found in the library. I also found some by Pat Conroy."

"Guy loved his books. He even met Pat Conroy in person on a few occasions. There are a few signed copies of his books in there, as well as some Mickey Spillane. You know he lived in Murrells Inlet," Hannah said.

As Hannah and Pauly segued into a discussion on books by authors who currently or once lived in South Carolina, Theo turned to the cook.

"Sugar, I'm gonna be here all day. We'll have three guests for supper tonight. I'm going to prepare a special low-country meal for them," Maralyn replied.

Finally, it was her turn. "I have no plans to go anywhere."

"No running off with the first deputy that shows up at the door?"

Peri made a face at him. "No. No running off with anyone. What about you?"

"I'm not going anywhere, either. I brought my laptop so I can work from here."

Pauly looked at Theo and winked. "And maybe squeeze in a nap, too."

Theo laughed. "Maybe."

Peri smiled. The two were obviously sharing some secret.

Looking around the table, Peri's smile grew. The warmth of the people surrounding her was palpable. Every one of them cared about the others. She was a lucky woman to be a part of the group. Together, they had saved her life.

Alva and Verdita walked through the kitchen door to begin their cleaning day. It was seven-fifty, and still no sign of Bambi.

Peri refused to spend the morning thinking about it. If Bambi didn't make an appearance by one PM for lunch, she would deal with her.

"If anyone needs me, I'll be in my office." After carrying her dirty dishes to the sink and refilling her coffee mug, Peri went upstairs.

Peri checked the clock on the computer. It was nearly time for lunch. She didn't know if Bambi had left her room yet or not. Time to find out.

After walking through the hall, she knocked on room number two.

"What do you want?" Bambi asked groggily.

"You have to get up and dress. It's almost lunchtime," Peri called back.

"Just send me up a plate," Bambi responded.

Now Peri was losing her patience and getting angry. "That won't be happening. If you're not downstairs to join us for lunch in thirty minutes, you won't get any. You also need to make plans to either return home tomorrow or find somewhere else to stay, because tonight is the last night you'll be staying here." Not waiting for a response, Peri headed downstairs.

Maralyn looked up from the vegetables she was preparing for a salad. "I ain't seen that woman yet."

"Don't worry. I just stopped by her room and gave her some ultimatums." Peri related to the cook what she'd told Bambi. "Where's Grannah?"

Maralyn nodded her head toward the pool patio. "She and Pauly are sittin' out there readin'. How they can stand that heat's beyond me."

Peri walked to the bank of windows. She looked across the shaded porch. Alva had put up the four umbrellas around the pool. Hannah and Pauly reclined in chaises on opposite sides of one of them. Each had a book in their hands. Jigger was stretched out by her grandmother's feet, watching the yard for invaders.

Peri set the table while Maralyn finished the meal preparations. Everyone showed up just before one—except Bambi. Just when Peri feared Dean would have to toss her out, Bambi stalked into the kitchen-den area.

Bambi yanked out an empty chair and threw herself into it. "I'm here. I should be resting. Yesterday was very traumatic for me." She glared at Peri. "You, of all people, should be more sympathetic."

Hannah stared across the table, her brown eyes flashing. "I have had enough of your rudeness. My granddaughter did not have to invite you here, but she felt sorry for you. Now you will either behave like an adult instead of a petulant child, or you can pack your bags and leave this instant."

Bambi stared at Hannah in shock. A moment later, her gaze dropped. "Will someone pass the salad, please?"

To hide her grin, Peri looked down at her plate.

After an abnormally quiet lunch, Bambi excused herself to take a walk. She left the backyard, following the path toward the pond and the graveyard.

Helen Marr, the last guest for the weekend, arrived a little after four. The petite septuagenarian was a delight. She wrote historical romance and had come to do research on her current book. That was Hannah's favorite genre, just inching out mysteries. Helen and Hannah became instant friends.

The Clines from their foray around six. By seven, everyone sat down to supper, including a subdued Bambi. They all enjoyed a scrumptious meal of local seafood and vegetables. For dessert, Pauly had made a peach cobbler with some of the last peaches of the season. Maralyn served it hot with homemade ice cream melting on top.

By the time they finished the leisurely meal, the sun was going down. Maralyn finished in the kitchen and headed home. Everyone else moved to the more comfortable seating in the living room. While most of them stayed to enjoy the conversation, Bambi went upstairs to her room. After a while, the rest gradually separated and headed for their beds.

Peri was exhausted. It had been a good day but a tiring one. With the exception of Bambi, their guests were enjoying themselves. Happy guests meant repeat customers and good word-of-mouth advertising. So far, they had been lucky with their burgeoning B&B endeavor.

Between the earnings from it, including Dean's and Theo's apartment rentals and Pauly's seemingly permanent room rental, combined with the farm rental for crops, they wouldn't have any trouble paying their bills.

Peri had just finished washing her face and brushing her teeth when someone knocked frantically on her bedroom door. Thinking one of the guests needed something, she hurried to answer.

One did. Only it wasn't the one she expected.

"Peri, I need your help. I just realized that I lost my bracelet. Jason gave it to me, and it's all I have left of him. I've looked all over my room, and it's not there. I even checked the kitchen, the den, and the living area. I can only think I lost it earlier during my walk. But I don't want to go out there alone. And I need a flashlight."

Over Bambi's shoulder, Peri saw Jason and Sheila.

"I did give her a gold bracelet a year or so ago. She's not wearing it," Jason said, earning an annoyed stare from Sheila.

Peri didn't want to go, but it would be easier to spot a bracelet at night in the beam of a flashlight than during the day. After slipping her feet into sneakers, Peri left her room, closing the door behind her.

"Come on. Let's get this over with." Peri led Bambi to the utility closet off the family room. Grabbing two flashlights, she handed one to Bambi. With the other woman on her heels, Peri exited through the family room door, crossed the pool patio, and followed the cement walk to the side gate. There, she flicked on the flashlight and began playing the beam back and forth across the oyster shell path.

Moving up beside her, Bambi did the same. "I hope we find it soon. I don't like it out here at night. That gray stuff hanging from the trees is creepy. And the noise is crazy."

"It's called Spanish moss. Most people find it romantic." Being out here after dark didn't bother Peri. She'd grown up exploring the land both day and night. "And most of the noise is from frogs and crickets."

"Well, I don't like it. And I don't think it's romantic."

"How far did you walk?"

"To that creepy old cemetery. As soon as I got to the gate, I turned around."

Peri hoped they didn't have to walk that far. There was an oppressiveness to the air that hinted a storm might be on the way. As if to prove her right, lightning flashed to the west. But was it a storm or just heat lightning? She didn't hear thunder, but it might be too distant.

Beside her, Bambi jumped. "What was that?"

"Lightning. It's not close."

A Barred owl called from a nearby tree.

Squawking, Bambi grabbed Peri's arm. "What was that?"

Peri told her. "There are a lot of wild animals who live in these woods."

"Can we hurry?"

"Sure, but we may miss spotting your bracelet." Peri didn't expect Bambi to find it, anyway. The woman was too busy looking for monsters in the trees and shrubs.

Releasing Peri's arm, Bambi began searching the ground again. She picked up the pace to the point that she was almost trotting.

Peri was okay with that. The sooner they recovered the bracelet, the sooner they could return to the house.

They weren't far from the graveyard. The split in the trail was right in front of them. Raising the beam of her flashlight, Peri shone it ahead. The cemetery fence came into view. After a few more steps, they could see the gate.

Something sparkled as the beam of light struck it. "I think we found it." Walking up to the gate, Peri frowned when she got a good look at it. It hung from one of the metal picket finials. Unbroken. Someone had deliberately placed it there. No way had it fallen off Bambi's wrist.

"Peri, look out!" Jason shouted. *"Amy's here."*

"Okay, I brought her," Bambi said simultaneously. "I'm heading back to the house."

"I'm afraid I can't let you do that." Amy stepped from behind an oak, a revolver in her right hand. "Your part in this isn't over yet."

A shot rang out.

Bambi went down.

Peri turned off her flashlight and ducked behind the nearest tree.

This wasn't good. She was in the woods with a madwoman. Peri had to keep Amy from shooting her until the cavalry arrived. Someone at the house had to have heard the report of the gun.

"You can't hide from me forever, Peri," Amy called out.

Wanna bet, Peri thought to herself.

A few hundred yards away, startled by the sound, a bobcat screamed. The shot had stirred up the local fauna.

The Barred owl screeched again as it flew. Another shot rang out. Peri hoped Amy hadn't shot the owl. She wanted to look, but she didn't dare.

"That owl swooped down over her head," Sheila told her. *"Scared the you-know-what outta her."*

"Put your weapon down, Amy." Theo's voice boomed out of the darkness.

Peri looked in the direction of his voice but couldn't see him. Which was a good thing because Amy fired in his direction. Peri wasn't that familiar with guns, but she knew a revolver when she saw one. If she hadn't missed counting one because of her fear, Amy had three shots left. Theo probably knew that. She hoped he did. If she tried to warn him, Amy would know precisely where she was.

"Put the gun down, Amy. I won't ask again. The police have been called. They're on their way."

While Peri felt as if she was hyperventilating, Theo didn't even sound out of breath.

Amy fired another shot. Then someone was running away.

Peri squeaked as Theo appeared out of the darkness. "Stay here. Or better yet, if you can get in the cemetery without the gate making a racket, do that. Hide among the stones until I return."

Peri grabbed his arm. "Stay here. Let the police deal with her."

"I can't, sweetheart. I don't want her to escape again." Cupping her cheek in his free hand, Theo gave her a quick kiss. She barely had time to return it before he disappeared back into the shadows.

Though the moon was a few nights past full, it wasn't yet high enough to be shining down through the trees. The oyster shell path gleamed dully in what light managed to filter through. Beneath the branches of the trees, it was pitch black. Though Peri still held the flashlight, she wasn't about to turn it on.

Peri peered around the tree trunk. Several feet away, she could make out Bambi's shape on the side of the path. "Why am I not seeing Bambi's ghost?" she whispered.

"You're asking me? I don't know. I don't even know why you're seeing me," Jason responded.

"Don't look at me. I don't have a clue. We're just as much in the dark as you are. No pun intended," Sheila added.

"Well, I'm not moving. I'm going to stay right here until Theo gets back." Peri didn't want to go into the cemetery. Though it was a familiar place that held no fear for her, she felt she could be trapped if she entered the fenced enclosure.

CHAPTER TWENTY

Assured that Peri was unharmed, Theo took off after the murderer. Amy didn't have much of a start on him, and his legs were longer. He didn't know how she'd gotten on the property without someone seeing her. What he knew was that she would not get away this time.

Amy's death toll was up to three. Theo planned to make sure there wasn't a fourth.

Following her was proving more difficult than he'd expected. He couldn't just run straight up on her because she had two more bullets, and he didn't know how good a shot she was.

Theo didn't grow up in the country. He was a city suburb kid who assumed it was quiet in the country. Maybe it was in the plains states, but here near the coast, the night was alive with a raucous cacophony of frogs, crickets, birds, and other night creatures. It made it difficult, nearly impossible, to hear Amy's movements.

And in the deep shadows, movement was hard to discern.

As much as he could, Theo stayed in the softer area of grass and moss at the edge of the path.

Amy tried to do the same, but she didn't know the area like he did. At least, Theo didn't think she did. Every so often, she ran on the path, and he heard the shells crunch beneath her shoes.

Pauly had given him some sort of kitchen twine to use to tie her up. Theo tucked his pistol into his back waistband and grabbed the length of thin rope. He was gaining on her. He just had to get her down without either of them getting shot.

Close enough now to see her trotting stealthily ahead of him, Theo increased his speed. Hoping her gun wouldn't go off, Theo made a flying tackle that would have made his high school football coach shout with joy.

Not only did the gun she carried not go off, but when she hit the ground, it flew out of her hand. Using his weight to help subdue her, Theo quickly tied her hands behind her back. Leaving her on the ground, he retrieved her weapon before going back to her.

Amy squirmed and flopped like a landed fish. After he jerked her to her feet, she tried to kick him and even bite him. Theo laughed. She might believe she was tough, but she was an angry toddler compared to the evil people he'd dealt with overseas.

"Give it up. Why don't you at least try to make things easier on yourself?" Theo suggested.

"Why should I? What do I have to lose now? I already lost the only thing I ever wanted. Jason was supposed to be mine forever. He was mine!"

"Amy, people don't treat people they love like possessions. Jason wasn't some ornament for you to display and hold on to."

"He betrayed me. We took sacred vows, and he broke them."

"Jason said you betrayed him, too."

Her head snapped around to stare at him. "When did he tell you that?" When he remained silent, she said, "What I did didn't count because I was only doing it to make him jealous." She narrowed her eyes. "He told Peri, didn't he? I knew they were having an affair no matter what she said. And I would have gotten her sooner, but I couldn't get close. I had to use Bambi to lure her out here."

"Peri and Jason were never lovers. Ever. That was all in your head. And maybe Jason's."

Amy snorted out a laugh. "So you say. I know better. At least I got two of the three. And I almost got Peri, too."

Amy had lost her grip on reality—if she'd ever had one in the first place.

In the distance, Theo heard the wail of approaching sirens. The quiet night at Frog Knot was about to be brought to a wild end. He hoped it didn't make the three guests decide to leave. Or worse, leave bad reviews when they did.

He couldn't worry about that now. He had to get back to Peri and walk both her and Amy back to the house. Then he'd have to bring someone out to process the scene and retrieve Bambi's body.

Theo didn't have a flashlight. Neither did Amy, except perhaps a cell phone one. At least the moon was bright enough to light the shell pathway. Theo had no desire to step on a snake or run across a gator on a night hunt. Thankfully, it didn't take them long to reach the cemetery. As they stopped by the gate, some sirens whined to a stop. Others could still be heard approaching.

Pauly knew the direction they'd come. Soon, officers would head their way.

"Peri!" he called. He tightened his grip on Amy's arm as she began to struggle. As movement came from in front of him instead of within the cemetery, he reached for his gun. Recognizing Peri, he brought his hand back around.

Aiming it toward the ground, Peri turned her flashlight on.

Theo walked toward her, tugging a still-struggling Amy along with him. "Get behind me on my left." He wanted Peri on the opposite side from Amy. The woman was still fighting him, and he didn't want her to have a chance to go after Peri.

Peri did as he asked. Moving off to his left and slightly behind. She kept the beam of the flashlight on the ground ahead of them.

They barely walked a few yards when they heard people running toward them. Moments later, they saw lights bobbing through the leaves.

"Over here!" Theo called. He didn't want anyone to be startled in the dark. Especially not people armed with guns.

Four deputies, followed closely by Jake and Dalton, bounded up the path. Theo recognized two of the deputies and the detective.

"Theo, what's going on here? Is that Amy Hughes?" The detective was the first one to reach them.

"Yes, she murdered a woman named Bambi Booza. Before you ask, that is her real name," Theo said.

Amy called Bambi a rude name.

Theo shoved the woman toward the deputies. "Can one of you please take her? Just don't underestimate her. She already informed me she has nothing to lose."

The detective nodded to two of the accompanying deputies. They stepped forward and took Amy off his hands. They immediately exchanged the rope for handcuffs. Once they had her secured, they led her off.

"We only know of Jason Hughes and Sheila Wright. You're telling me there is a third victim?"

"Nearly a fourth. She tried to kill Peri, too."

Peri stepped up beside Theo. As she slipped her hand into his, he closed his fingers around hers. "Amy shot Bambi a short while ago. She's down the trail near the cemetery." Peri began to shake.

Releasing her hand, Theo put his arm around her and hugged her to his side. "I need to get her to the house. She's going into shock."

"I can show you where the cemetery is," Jake offered.

The detective nodded to Theo. "Go ahead. We'll catch up with you later."

That's all Theo needed to hear. He headed for the house. Dalton went with them, walking on Peri's other side. Theo appreciated his friend's thoughtfulness.

They saw the lights before they reached the fenced yard. Floodlights were on, driving the night shadows back. The porch and loggia lights were also on, and through the screens of the loggia, they could see flashing lights from first responder vehicles.

Alton sat on the end of a chaise on the patio next to Hannah, Pauly, and the three guests. Dean, pacing nearby, ran to meet them the moment he spotted them. Throwing his arms around them, he hugged them both.

Alton, Hannah, and Pauly got to their feet. As soon as Dean released them, Peri headed straight for her grandmother. Because she didn't run, Hannah's expression of fear calmed. When they embraced, they held on as if they'd never let go.

Alton walked over and clapped Theo on the shoulder. "I hate to do this, son, but I've now got two people in custody for murder. I need you and Peri to come down to the station and give your statements tonight while the events are fresh."

Theo nodded. It wasn't as if they'd be able to go to sleep anytime soon, anyway. They might as well put their time to good use and get the interviews out of the way.

"Fine, but Peri's a bit shocky. She's going to need some orange juice or something with sugar."

"I'll put some orange juice in a thermal mug." Dean headed for the kitchen.

"You've also got another body," Theo informed the sheriff. "Amy shot Bambi Booza. Jake is taking the detective and the deputy to the scene now. They've probably already called for your CSI team."

"Seems we're going to have a lot to talk about." Alton's gaze glued on the path for a few seconds.

After giving Peri enough time to reassure her grandmother that she was unharmed and for Dean to supply her with a container of cold orange juice, Alton bundled her and Theo into his sedan and drove them to department headquarters.

CHAPTER TWENTY-ONE

The sun had been up several hours by the time Peri and Theo were driven back to Frog Knot. Everyone, including the three guests, was waiting to hear the particulars of what had transpired the previous night.

Once they were all seated in the den, Peri and Theo took turns filling them in.

"Bambi got Peri out of the house on the pretext of finding a lost bracelet. Amy was waiting at the cemetery to shoot Peri," Theo said.

Hannah put a hand to her chest. "You didn't tell me that."

"I'm fine, Grannah. I ducked behind a tree because I got a warning. Bambi didn't."

"So, Amy killed all of them?" Dean asked.

Theo exchanged glances with Peri before saying, "We're not sure. She killed Jason and Bambi. We know that, but there is some question whether she or Bambi killed Sheila. Amy is claiming Bambi did that one."

Peri picked it up there. "According to Amy, when she got wind of the divorce, she went to the office and confronted Bambi, but Bambi knew nothing about the divorce. She mentioned it to Jason, and he tried to deny it. That's when Bambi got suspicious that she wasn't the one he was leaving Amy for. She did some digging and discovered Sheila. Of course, Amy still thought it was me Jason was having an affair with. She just wouldn't let it go."

"You were his first love," Theo said. "She knew that. And every woman he was involved with resembled you. Amy had to see that. In her eyes, even if you hadn't had an affair with him, you were still in her way."

Dean shook his head. "How did Bambi and Amy get together?"

Theo looked at Peri and waited for her to tell them. "When Bambi discovered Jason was coming to the area to meet Sheila, she went to Amy and suggested they team up and try to break them up. I don't believe she thought Amy would kill Jason."

Theo nodded. "I don't think she planned to kill him. She told me he was all she ever wanted. I think he said or did something that sent her over the edge. Once she'd killed him, there was no turning back. I believe she killed Sheila, too, but we'll probably never know for certain."

"So where did she kill Jason? It wasn't in the hotel room, was it?" Pauly asked.

Peri looked at Theo.

"No. She killed him at his parent's old house. Though it showed in someone else's name, Jason hadn't sold it yet. She lured him there, and when whatever happened to send her over happened, she stabbed him with a kitchen knife. Then, realizing she needed to dispose of the body, she called a man she knew had been in love with her since high school. A man she'd already used to try to set Peri up at the hotel."

"Ricky Jackson," Hannah said.

Peri and Theo both nodded.

"When that didn't go as planned because Jason wasn't where they expected him to be, Amy went to Plan B. She didn't realize Jason was spending most of his time at Sheila's. When Amy found out was when she called him and lured him to the old farmhouse. Jason was too heavy for her to lift anyway, but they call it dead weight for a reason. A dead body is crazy heavy. Ricky helped her with that," Theo said.

Hannah shook her head. "Ricky came from a nice family. Now he's ruined his life, and all for a crazy woman who never loved him."

"What about...," Dean looked at the three guests, "...you know who?"

"I think they'll be leaving soon." Peri smiled.

Jason and Sheila stood near the porch door, patiently waiting for Peri to join them.

"This is the most exciting vacation I've ever had," Clara Cline told her husband. Her expression wavered between excitement and shock.

Peri knew how she felt.

"A little too much for me. But don't worry, Peri; we'll definitely come and stay here again. Since we're leaving tomorrow, we're going to head down to Charleston for the rest of the day. We'll be back for supper." Roger stood and helped his wife to her feet. They headed for the back porch door and their car.

That made Peri feel much better. She hadn't been sure how they would react.

"I'd love to remain and hear more, but I'll have to get it later. I got the meeting with the historian I wanted, and I simply can't be late." Mrs. Marr rose and headed for her rental car.

"I think I'm going to take a walk before I come back and take a long nap," Peri said. She glanced at Theo as she stood.

"Mind if I join you?" Theo asked.

"I'd be delighted."

Leaving the rest of the household still talking about the murders, Peri led Theo outside and to the shell path. She walked toward the cemetery.

"Thank you for coming. I wanted to say goodbye to Jason and Sheila, and I didn't want to do it with a big audience."

"No problem." After a bit, he asked, "Are they with us?"

"Yes. Sheila asked if I'd go with them to the cemetery. They like it there."

They were quiet as they walked through the live oaks and other trees. A gentle breeze carrying humid air caressed their skin and ruffled their hair. Peri hoped that with their murder, or possibly murderers, caught, the spirits could finally find peace.

Peri stopped just outside the cemetery gate as Jason and Sheila passed through it.

He pointed to the bracelet still hanging from the fence. *"Would you throw that in the river for me?"*

Peri nodded. "I'd be glad to."

"Thank you, Peri, for helping us get justice," Sheila said. *"We're going to be fine now. We can see the light, and this time, we'll be able to go through it."*

Jason nodded. *"Thank you. You always were too good for me."* He looked at Theo. *"I think maybe you've found your other half just as I found mine."* Jason smiled down at a beaming Sheila. *"Goodbye, Peri."* He turned back to face her as he and Sheila began to fade.

This time, when they both disappeared, Peri knew they wouldn't return. They had found their peace, and she was happy she'd been able to help them. She removed the bracelet from where it hung.

Theo turned her to face him. "Are you okay? You're crying."

Peri brushed her cheeks with her free hand, surprised to discover they were wet. "I'm fine. They've found peace now. I just need to do one more thing for Jason."

Together, she and Theo walked back and took the path to the river. When Peri handed the bracelet to Theo, he threw it way out into the river. They watched it sink into the depths.

Theo took her hand, and they walked back to the house.

THE END

ACKNOWLEDGMENTS

M y parents were, of course, the largest influence in my life. They were both older when I was born (as in 59 and 40 just a few months later). Both read voraciously and read to me. We traveled together, most often to historical sites. Dad and Mom loved history. They loved many genres of books, including mysteries. They started me on my path to becoming a writer.

Then there were my grandparents. I only knew three of them, my paternal grandfather having died before my parents married. Both grandmothers were strong women, and I'd like to think that the reader sees a bit of them in my heroines. My maternal grandfather encouraged my storytelling. We would take long walks and collect rocks as we went. We would make up stories about them, and he saved the rocks.

There are so many others. Teachers who encouraged me. Friends who kept telling me I should write down the stories I told them at recess. Close friends who support me. Other friends who have moved past being just friends to the point of being my chosen family of the heart.

I couldn't do this without them, and I hope they know it.

Check out the song, "No Charge," sung by Caro Emerald. This gave me the idea for the opening of the book.

Hannah's Tomato Pie

5-6 large tomatoes

1 C mayo

¾ C grated onion

1 C (or more) grated cheese (we like sharp cheddar), plus extra for the top

1 unbaked pie shell

Slice tomatoes. Allow them to drain a little. Then fill an unbaked pie shell with them.

Mix together mayo with grated onion, and 1 cup grated cheese. Spread on top of the tomatoes. When done, sprinkle more of the grated cheese over the top.

Bake 350° for thirty minutes or until crust is golden brown. Rich but good.

Feel free to add bacon bits, parsley, or anything else you like.

Don't miss out!

Visit the website below and you can sign up to receive emails whenever Sloane McClain publishes a new book. There's no charge and no obligation.

https://books2read.com/r/B-A-UMNJ-EYUOC

Connecting independent readers to independent writers.

About the Author

Sloane has always loved mysteries. The first "book" she ever wrote was a mystery. Though at age eight, the "book" was only around twelve pages long. She's finally combining her love of mysteries, the paranormal, and some Southern charm in this new paranormal, cozy mystery series.

Sloane currently has two very spoiled rescue dogs. She also loves photography. You'll often find her photographs on her social media pages.

You can contact her on Facebook: SloaneMcClainAuthor

BookBub: @SloaneMcClain

BlueSky @ sloanemcclain.bsky.social

Instagram: @pendragonsandhunters

Pendragonsandhunters@gmail.com

Milton Keynes UK
Ingram Content Group UK Ltd.
UKHW041822211123
432980UK00001BB/131